Spindrift Love

Spindrift Love

JOCELYN HOLST BOLSTER

atmosphere press

Published by Atmosphere Press

Cover design by Kevin Stone

Atmospherepress.com

To Mom, who taught me to dance before I could walk.

1

THE COLOR OF BOURBON

I was born in Bourbon County, just on the Kansas side of the border with Missouri. I thought it was funny that it was called Bourbon County when I found out what bourbon meant because it's a dry county. That means there's no liquor. Not sold in stores nor served in restaurants. That was just fine with my parents since Dad was a minister in the Kansas Reformed Church and Mom was a minister's wife. There was no drinking, smoking, dancing, rock music, or Santa Claus.

But our house was full of love.

Mom. She was the sweetest girl in four counties. That's what everybody said. Grandpa said the people of Independence wept the day she married Dad and moved away. All the way out here in the middle of nowhere. Had to go where they were called, they said. Kansas is spread out like a patchwork quilt. Wheat fields and sunflowers in the west—flatter than a pancake. Then, moving east, slow cracks in the dry earth become brownish, tan bluffs that rise up and follow shallow streams formed by spring runoff of winter ice and snow. The sweeping farms, so big you can't see the other edge of the field, give way to endless cattle grounds with sparse patches of trees clustered around mostly dried-up creeks. At the edge of the cattle grounds, as you're about to leave Kansas and enter the beauty of the Ozarks in Missouri, is a heavily forested area. Right on that edge of the vast emptiness and tremendous range, is where we lived.

It was a small house on a thirsty, triangle-shaped piece of wildness. We were in front of the Richardson's cattle ranch to the north, next to a small creek that ran down from the ranch and joined with another small creek at the southeast corner, and right behind the railroad tracks to the south. Now, when I say in front of the cattle ranch, I mean I would have to walk a good hour to reach the closest house. But when I say right behind the tracks, I mean it. They ran diagonal through the front yard. Close enough to spit on, if spitting were something anyone in our house could conceive to do. Close enough to hop right on and fade into the half-light of ascension.

To someone from a city I guess it would have been easy to feel lonely out there, but it never occurred to me. Sometimes I felt sad and I didn't know for what. Maybe the empty space around me crept in a bit too close. Maybe I wasn't paying close enough attention to notice that it wasn't really empty. Whatever the reason, when I felt like that, I'd ask Mom to braid my hair. Her hands, tugging softly at the knots, making everything smooth and beautiful. That's what she did best.

That's what we were doing that afternoon. It was the first warm day we had had since last fall. Winter lasted all the way until the end of school that year. Gray and dry with a wind that bit. And it was boring. Almost no snow. Every day looked the same: brown earth and gray sky, like a photograph before there was color. Finally, at the beginning of summer break, a warm wind blew in. It blew away the dull ceiling and blue appeared; a blue so deep it was shocking, almost too bright. A blue that made me imagine the ocean. The sun shone on the brown, crunchy grass for a day and green appeared. Just like that. And it was like I was seeing green for the very first time—not that year, but for the first time ever.

Mom and I sat on the front porch and let the breeze touch our bare arms. She slid her fingers through my long hair and we waited for the sun tea to brew. Mom made tea the old-fashioned way by letting the sun heat the water set out on the stoop.

We weren't talking and we could hear a train coming up in the distance. It slowed before it reached our yard and creaked in real soft. It was one that was going to stop for a while so the engine come up real slow next to the house and I waved at the engineer like a kid. Then the freight cars came in, moaning and yawning, and settled in like a giant, steel wall, blocking our view of the row of cottonwoods at the far end of the yard. The rhythm of the click clacks came to a stop, then the rhythm of Mom's hands in my hair stopped, then the rocker Mom was sitting in stopped and everything was perfectly still.

Trains came by day and night, blowing that long, sad whistle across the plains and shaking our little house on its foundation. But I only ever noticed them when they stopped. Sometimes a train would have to stop for a switch up ahead and it would just set there in front of the house. When I was little Mom got real worried about me playing on the tracks, trying to squish pennies or laying my ear down on the rail to listen for a train coming from far off, straining to hear a whisper from those other worlds, but she never got worried about the hobos and transients that rode the rails.

Freight hoppers, they called themselves. A long time ago before I was born they were worn out but hardworking men who were down on their luck, wandering from state to state, looking for work or comfort or a dream, carving up the landscape with their hobo songs and making the long, stubborn, deserted places on the prairie mean something. But now they were mostly college kids or high school dropouts who'd learned about the hobo life on the Internet.

Still, if one got off and came toward the house, Mom figured he had to have been called by God to wander up to this particular house to share in our particular fellowship and find his way before riding the rails back home. Even after the time the hobo pulled a knife on Dad, Mom still believed in the goodness of all people and in the beauty and grace of God.

But beauty is subjective. And grace is often hard to see.

Mom didn't know it, but this was going to be my last summer at home. Next year was my senior year and I was planning on leaving right after graduation. It sounds like a normal thing to do, but I was only fifteen. Mom and Dad wanted to keep me home as long as they could. The Fort Scott community college was only a half hour's drive away, and Dad had plans for me to get my associate's degree and take over as the church choir director for Mrs. Carlson who'd been ready to retire for a few years. We had to be practical. We didn't have the money for me to go to a real college, or to move away. He even hinted that I might meet a nice boy in the Christian Youth Fellowship there and go on to marry a minister. But getting married didn't seem interesting or even practical to me. If he had asked, I'd have told him that I wanted to go somewhere near the ocean, study real music. See something...else. Put my feet in the sand near the sea. I felt the patchwork quilt of home pressing on me, scratching and suffocating. This would be my last summer at home, the summer the freight hopper stayed for a while—the summer of Cody, the last summer of my innocence.

Mom tugged at my hair, separating it into three parts. Puffs of cottonwood seeds snowed down and landed on the still train cars. Mom sneezed.

"Bless you."

"This cottonwood gets me every year," she said. "I wish

something else would start blooming. I'd even be happy if the weeds would blossom!"

"No you wouldn't," I said.

"You're right. I wouldn't," she laughed. "You'll help me weed the garden this summer, won't you, Jesse? If it ever grows."

"Sure." I glanced over at the brown square, barely held together by a raggedy fence, that Mom called a garden. It looked like dandelions were already starting to take over. I shuddered thinking about pulling them. I shuddered again thinking about pulling them forever and ever until the day the Lord took me amen like Mom was doing. "Mom," I asked somberly, "was there a feeling you had when you realized that you were a woman? I mean, like a real, woman grown?"

Her hands paused for a moment and hung heavily in my braid.

"That's a tricky question, Jesse." She took up the braid again. "I suppose I thought I was pretty grown up when I went to the prom with Rocky Hendricks. He borrowed his mom's truck and we drove around the back roads so fast..."

I could hear her smiling as she told it—the same story I'd heard a hundred times about her prom.

"We broke down out on the far edge of my daddy's farm before we even got to the dance. He was so sweet," she laughed, "he turned the radio up and we—well, we listened to the music right there in the fields. Milo, it was. Just turning green." She sighed and picked up a rubber band. "But I definitely wasn't grown up yet. Come to think of it, that was probably the last time I was truly young." Her hands left my hair altogether. I turned to see her gazing out at the train cars. She twisted my head back around and tugged out the braid she had just finished.

"I figured a woman has to be grown up when she gets married. But that certainly is not the case," she continued.

"Here's what I think, Jesse: One morning, when you were just a tiny little thing, you had been awake every hour of the night for weeks. It felt like I hadn't slept in months. Hadn't really, you were colicky. But this one particular morning, I had just gotten you back in your crib, after screaming all night, and Daddy let the door slam behind him on his way out to work."

My hair pulled at the edges of my scalp as she reformed three strands.

"I had just laid down and you let out a scream—well, I got up, and I fed you and I cleaned you and I read to you and sang to you—and I thought I was going to die from the sleep deprivation, I really did. But I got up and took care of you anyway and I guess, right then, I guess that's when I knew I was really grown."

She tied a rubber band around the end of my braid, which was so tight it hurt a little. Then she leaned down and kissed the top of my head.

"You know I wouldn't change a thing about you," she whispered. "Why are you asking—"

She was interrupted. Thankfully.

A man emerged from a crack in the door of one of the freight cars. He jumped off and stood there looking at us. There we were, completely alone, and suddenly a person was standing not twenty feet away. I wanted to jump up and run inside, but then I saw his eyes.

They were green. Like the new green that was sprouting up all around the plains. Maybe more green next to his tanned and dirty face. And, like the new green of that summer, it was like I was seeing the color for the first time.

He looked like your typical freight hopper at first—dirty and tired. Maybe trying to capture some lifestyle or philosophy that exists in a very real and certain splendor in their minds—but when he got closer I noticed he was different than the others. Most freight hoppers are running from something. We met one once who was on the run from the Army. Sometimes it's from their parents—or society in general. But this one, he looked more like he was running from a bad feeling.

He took a couple steps toward us and stopped. Mom stood up.

"Hi," he mumbled. And waved.

"Hello," Mom said back, her arms crossed over her chest, sizing him up. She believed in the goodness of all people, but she wasn't naive.

He just stood there in front of us, looking like a lost dog. Well, Mom loved that stray look. She uncrossed her arms and moved her hands to her hips. She pointed her chin toward the train car behind him.

"Did you hop off that rail for conversation?" She asked, cocking her head.

The hobo smiled, revealing straight, white teeth. The teeth of a kid whose parents can afford an orthodontist. I ran my tongue quickly across my crooked ones.

"Maybe you need a ride into Fort Scott?" Mom asked.

"Um," he reached up and rubbed the back of his head, squinting up at Mom, "I don't know." Mom raised her eyebrows at him. "Conversation, I guess?" He gave a look that wondered if that was okay.

A crooked smile I'd never seen swept across Mom's face and she shifted her weight onto one foot.

"Well, come on up," she said, motioning to the porch.

Most freight hoppers who came up to the house were driven there by desperation. It didn't happen often—sometimes years would go by without us seeing one—but when they visited us, they were desperate. The train stopped and they couldn't bring themselves to keep on going, so they jumped off the first chance they got. They didn't care where they ended up. Maybe the stifling loneliness or the constant movement or the fear of being out there in the dark all alone got to them and they had to jump. But this one looked like he wasn't quite sure if he wanted to get off yet. He walked toward the porch like a cow forced out of the barn on a frozen, winter morning. The train sighed a heavy, metallic lamentation and creaked forward on the tracks. He turned and looked at it with longing, like he might run and jump back on. But he watched it go and then turned back toward us.

As he got closer I could see how tall he was. Much taller than Dad. He was wearing an army-green T-shirt with a peace sign on it. He walked up the steps to the porch and looked me right in the eyes. It felt just like he had touched me.

"Stop!" I shouted. His eyes grew and he held up his palms like he was being arrested. I stooped down in front of him and picked up a cicada that had been struggling to molt on the steps the whole afternoon. I set it on the tree to the side of the porch. My cheeks burned and I looked off at the tail end of the train, cursing my fair skin that always gives me away. I reached up and yanked the braids out of my hair so fast it hurt. He kept looking.

Mom picked up the sun tea and paused at the door to take a long look at the hobo before going inside to get glasses and ice. She emerged a moment later with the good stuff, the glasses we use for company.

She poured out the tea—and her smile—for all of three of us. No one said a word. Sometimes, when you've been alone for a long time, you sort of forget how to talk to people, or you just get real lonely for the sound of human voices. When that happened to me I sang to myself. The hobo gulped down the tea in one, long swig, his Adam's apple moving up and down as he leaned his head back to get the last drops. I had to stop myself from humming to break the silence. Mom watched him with hawk eyes. She didn't touch her tea. He set the glass down like it was crystal and wiped his mouth with the back of his hand. Mom poured more tea.

"You sure are thirsty, hon," she said finally. "You been out on the rails for a long time?"

The hobo shrugged. "I guess it's been a while," he said, chugging down the second glass of tea. He set the empty glass down again and leaned back in the chair, letting his knees fall open and stretching his arms up behind his neck. That same crooked grin grew across Mom's face.

"How long has it been since you've eaten?" she asked, pouring another glass.

He looked up at Mom and smiled real big. "I guess it's been a while," he said, reaching for the tea.

Mom and I stood in the kitchen while the freight hopper sat on the front porch, drinking his fourth glass of tea.

"What are you doing?" I whispered.

"God works in mysterious ways, sweetheart," she whispered back, pulling food out of the pantry. "He might have been called to go on his journey, to come out here to us." She was checking the freezer for leftover ham or bacon. "Oh dear, I guess we'll have to make do with this." She pulled a lump of nameless tin foil out and set it in the sink to thaw. I swayed back on my heels and strained to see through the living room and out the front door to the porch. The freight hopper was turning the iced tea glass around in his hands. He looked up through the door and I twisted back out of sight.

"What if he's—I don't know. What if he's dangerous?" I said, leaning back to catch another glimpse, heart quickening. Mom paused.

"Well, you sound almost hopeful that he is," she said. "He's not dangerous, honey. I can tell." She went back to preparing the meal, and I went to the bathroom and brushed my hair. It was the one thing about me I considered pretty. Long and wavy. Brown with streaks of blonde here and there. It was the same as Mom's hair. I wished I had gotten her eyes too. I saw the way everyone melted when she looked at them. Grown men acting all funny and asking if we were sisters. At least I had the hair.

Mom put two casseroles in the oven and went outside to wait for Dad to come home. I waited in the kitchen, partially obscured by the wall that separated it from the living room, watching, listening, and pretending to set the table. I heard Dad rolling in down the old highway a good minute before the car came into view at the top of our driveway. Mom heard it too because she stood up and motioned to the hobo to stay put. Dad had taken the Brown Bomber to work that day. The car was from the eighties, the color of mud, and at least three times as loud as a normal car. You could hear it coming from a mile off. My heart beat annoyingly hard against my chest.

The Brown Bomber rumbled over the tracks and came to a stop in front of the garden patch. Dad emerged from the car wearing a suit and tie and a serious expression. That was his normal expression. Like he was on the verge of tears at all times. I moved into the living room and put a record on to get a closer listen. Schubert, "Serenade." It didn't matter how nervous or upset I ever got; music always brought me into serenity. Like the most safe, warm, comfortable room in heaven. Mom met Dad at the car door and said something I couldn't hear, then Dad moved up to the porch and without saying a word took the hobo's hands in his. He bowed his head in a silent prayer. The hobo raised his eyebrows.

"What's your name, son?" Dad said when he lifted his head.

"Sam," the rail hopper answered.

Dad ushered him into the living room while Mom cleaned up the tea glasses.

"Sam," Dad said, gearing up for a proper sermon. I could always tell by the tone of his voice. "This is a Christian household. There will be no smoking, swearing, drinking, or disrespect. If you can abide by those rules, then you are welcome to stay for dinner."

Sam's body turned rigid at Dad's words. I wondered for a moment what a non-Christian household was like. It may seem obvious that you shouldn't swear in the house of a preacher, but what Dad didn't tell Sam is that to him, swearing included words like *jeez* and *gosh* and *gal darn it*. And Dad didn't even mention dancing or rock music. Sam had to learn some of Dad's rules the hard way, just like I did.

Dad wasn't one of those booming preachers who could talk a congregation into salvation just by the power of his voice. He talked real low and deliberate and thoughtful. When he really wanted to make a point, he lowered his voice so much you had to strain and lean in to hear what he was saying. You had to make the entire room become completely still and silent. You had to almost hold your breath to hear him.

"Come," Dad half whispered. "Sit at our table and share in our fellowship."

Sam washed his hands then sat down right across from me. Dad took his place to my left. Mom set down a chicken-and-potato-chip casserole in the middle of the table, then sat down to my right. Schubert ended and a familiar silence filled the kitchen.

"Let us pray," Dad said. Sam looked like he fully anticipated this. He closed his eyes, bowed his head, and clasped his hands together in picture-perfect praying form.

But we hold hands during prayer at our table.

Mom reached out and gently touched his hand. He jumped in his chair and the metal legs made a scraping noise against the linoleum. I couldn't help but laugh. Mom though, in her tender way, just took hold of his hand and squeezed it tight. Then we closed our eyes. Dad had an audience, so he gave a particularly heartful prayer—and a long one. He said how thankful we were for this fellowship and the many hands that had brought this food to our table (even though it was mainly Mom), and the opportunity to meet new friends. I looked up to have a nice, long stare at Sam.

His eyes were open—and he was looking at Mom. His eyebrows were furrowed down a little bit, like he was thinking about something real hard as he looked over at her. She was still squeezing his hand with a tightness and tenderness that I knew well. She was so good at being strong and tender at the same time. He had long fingers and stubby nails—he must have bit them like me. When I turned my gaze from his hands back up to his face, he was looking at me. Then I jumped in my chair and scratched the linoleum. My breath caught in my throat. His eyes were so beautiful I almost couldn't look into them. He smiled real big and I could tell that underneath his calm expression he was ornery. That was the first time I learned that orneriness recognizes itself in others.

"And for all this we give thanks in the name of our lord and savior, Jesus Christ, amen."

"Amen."

"Now, let's dig in!" Dad said. He tried to sound fun sometimes, but it never quite worked. He always ended up sounding a bit too enthusiastic. Like the guy who sold us the Brown Bomber. "Tell us, Sam, where do you come from?"

"Oh, here and there," Sam said. If he was trying to sound mysterious, he succeeded. In a minute's time, my mind had evoked images of craggy mountaintops and misty forests and far away deserts. Here and there sounded like the most interesting place in the world.

"Well, you sound like you're from the east."

"You got me," Sam said. "I'm from Maine originally. Spent the last few years lobster fishing." He took a heaping portion of casserole.

"You take as much as you want, Sam. I made two casseroles," Mom chimed in.

"Thank you, ma'am," he smiled.

"Oh, you don't have to call me ma'am, honey."

"Lobster fishing–that's dangerous work," Dad said, like he'd ever even seen a lobster, or the ocean.

"It's not so bad," Sam said, piling food into his mouth.

"Not so bad? Well, I think you're just being modest, son. I knew a man, lost half his fingers lobster fishing."

"That can happen," Sam said, his mouth brimming with potato chips, cream of mushroom soup, and chicken.

"Heard of another one who went straight overboard in a storm," Dad said. I began to wonder where Dad had heard about all this.

"It pays well," Sam shrugged. "This is delicious casserole. Thank you for having me for dinner."

"You are very welcome." Mom's smile was huge.

"Very good meal, as usual," Dad said. "So, to you then, son, the good pay was worth risking your life?"

Sam cleared his plate with one last bite and set back from the table for a moment. I'd never seen anyone eat so fast. He swallowed.

"I wasn't out there for the pay," he said. "It's not really as dangerous as people think. Most people base their opinion about it on TV, but mostly it's really nice out on the sea. You go out for three months, then you have a few months off to travel, see the world. Most guys say the worst part isn't the danger but the boredom and the loneliness. You're out there sometimes just floating around, trying to find the catch, staring out at the open sea. Most guys start going crazy thinking about their girlfriends. But I always loved that part of it. That's why I did it. That's why I hopped on that train too. It's those moments, when you're all alone with yourself–" he paused and took a big, long breath and then half smiled, "It's those moments when you can really talk to God, ya know? When you find out what kind of man you are–on the inside."

With that comment he reached forward and helped himself to the last of the casserole.

Mom jumped up and got the other casserole out of the oven, humming to herself like she does when she's thinking over something. Dad shifted in his seat.

"You couldn't have spent much time out here in the Midwest then?" Dad asked.

Sam shook his head. "Just watched it go by. Today's the first time I actually set foot out here. I didn't mean to, really. I just..." he glanced at Mom setting another heap of food in front of him.

"What *are* you doing here, son?"

"What's the ocean like?" I blurted. "I mean," trying to sound casual, "what's it *like*?"

Sam looked at me and shrugged. "It's a lot of water," he said.

I sank in my seat and Dad eyed me suspiciously. Mom hummed her way over to the fridge.

Dad cleared his throat. "Well. It may not seem as exciting out here as being on a fishing boat, but you'll never find better folk. Salt of the earth. Enjoying the simple things God gave us."

"Sometimes it's exciting," Mom said, "remember that winter we spotted the cougar?" She stood behind Sam and scooped more food on his plate.

"That's right," Dad said. He lifted his plate. "I could use another helping."

"Oh, sure," Mom scootched the casserole dish toward Dad. "There you go."

"Thought it might run off with Jesse," Dad said. "She runs all over the prairie like a wild person, don't you, Jesse?" I froze. He started to chuckle to himself. "Remember that one time–what were you doing, hunting for frogs or something?"

"Not this story, Dad," I said through clenched teeth.

"That's our tomboy, Jesse," Mom said cheerfully. "She stays outside all day."

"She was out back. Somewhere beyond the ridge."

"I was just out walking, don't matter where."

"It *doesn't* matter where, honey."

"When she come tearin' round the corner like someone lit a fire under her. Naked as the day God made her."

"That was like, ten years ago. And I was wearing overalls."

"She had to do her *business* and didn't want to take the time to come in to go to the little girls' room, and, what was it Jesse, a deer?"

"It wasn't *like* ten years ago, honey. It *was* ten years ago."

"It was a coyote. It wasn't no deer."

"Wasn't *a* deer, honey."

"A deer come up on her when she was out there in the woods and spooked her so bad she didn't take the time to pull up her pants! Just ran home with the bottoms off!"

"I was only five years old. It was a *humongous* coyote."

Dad was in full hysterics, face red, eyes watering. He leaned to one side and pulled a handkerchief out of his back pocket to wipe his eyes. Sam and Mom had started to laugh from the contagion of it. Sam threw his head back and laughed with an open mouth. Dear Lord, why did his teeth have to be so perfectly straight?

"Humongous isn't a word, honey," Mom said, sighing her laughter away. "Say *very big* instead."

Dad's chest heaved as he wiped his eyes. Then he turned to me, "But seriously, Jesse." His smile was gone and he looked at me with solemn, red eyes. "You can't be a tomboy forever, climbing trees, hunting frogs. It's time you started acting like a young lady."

Sam, whose laughter had started dying down, snorted at this comment. Dad shot him a hard-nosed look and just like that he silenced the kitchen and sent out a wave of shame toward Mom and Sam for ever having laughed in the first place. Sam lowered his eyes and sat still; hands folded in his lap. The clock tick from the living room sounded like each second lasted a minute. I focused on the sound of the scratch of the record needle, rhythmically pulsing since Schubert side B had ended, and felt my body begin to shake.

"Maybe you should take some lessons from your mom," Dad said. My throat closed up just as if I was being choked. "Why don't you come down to the church with me tomorrow and help Mrs. Carlson with the hymnals? She could use a hand. You can see what a fun job it is."

Sure, may as well start helping Mrs. Carlson now because that's what I'll be doing the rest of my livelong days. Why wait to begin the march to the grave?

"Oh, that would be nice, honey," Mom chimed in. "Our Jesse has a beautiful singing voice," Mom explained to Sam. "Marcy Carlson is our choir director. You could practice some songs with her, Jesse." She heaped a giant spoonful of casserole on my plate.

"Or carry some boxes of hymnals up from the basement," Dad said. "You know who has a lovely voice? That classmate of yours, little Sophie Whatshername. I heard her the other day singing with the choir. She's grown into such a lovely young lady. Voice of an angel."

I shoved a heapful of food into my mouth and swallowed hard.

"Slow down, Jesse," Dad raised his eyebrows at me. "You want to have a figure like your mom, don't you?"

I set my fork down on my plate and stared at the casserole dish.

"I'd love to hear you sing," Sam interrupted, leaning over his plate to scoop up all the remaining chips and looking up at me. Air filled my lungs.

"I'm going to help Missy with her wedding this summer,"

I said matter-of-factly, crossing my arms over my chest. The room went still. Dad lowered his fork and got a look on his face like his dog just died. Mom stopped clearing the table and stood there, staring at the plate in her hand. Sam looked up from his plate, fork halfway to his mouth, like he just realized he'd been sitting in a den of sleeping lions this whole time and we all woke up.

"Missy wanted me to ask you if you'll officiate," I broke the silence.

"What?" Dad asked and I finally breathed out. "I thought they were getting married at JP's church. At the Catholic church," he said.

"They were," I explained, "but then the priest told them they were pure sin for, well, for you know, and that they had to take some classes and confess to being pure sin and then Missy would have to convert, and she just doesn't want to do all that."

Dad started to mumble under his breath. "Catholics. *Pure* sin." He pushed the casserole around his plate with his fork. He looked up at me. "Your mother and I don't think it's a good idea for you to be hanging around Missy so much anymore. Planning this wedding as if it's a perfectly normal thing to do."

I hated it when he brought Mom into the conversation to add to his authority when she hadn't even said anything. I looked at Sam, who was sitting very still and looking around the kitchen at nothing–at anything but us. Probably wondering when the next train come through so he could jump back on. And he'd be right. What was a boy like him doing in our kitchen anyway?

"Can I be excused?" I asked.

Dad took a breath.

"*May* I be excused, and sure, dear," Mom answered for him.

I picked up my plate and circled the table to take it to the sink. As I passed Sam, I took a long sniff, hoping I could commit his smell to memory. Dirt and sweat and rail grease and something I couldn't put a pin on. I pictured him standing on the bow of a boat, hauling in a net. Lobsters and oceans and seeing the world—I couldn't let myself think about it too long. Because I'd never see it. Just like the back of Sam's neck, strong and tan. I'd probably never see another boy like him, but at least I'd seen this one.

"Bye Sam," I said. He started to turn toward me but I couldn't stand to look at those green eyes again. I took off out the screen door.

I heard Sam's low voice say something and Mom giggle in the distance.

Behind our house, to the north, the creek had managed to carve out a tiny rut in the plateau. It started out as nothing by our house but grew wide enough for trees to grow and almost remind you of a canyon the further on it went onto the Richardson's property. Every kid has a place they go that's just theirs. Of course, it's probably not just theirs. Probably some kid had that spot before them and probably some kid will find it after they leave, but for a moment of time it's theirs. For me, it was an abandoned barn that sat nestled down in the canyon next to the creek. I found it about a mile away from my house, just as soon as I was old enough to go out wandering on my own. It was perfect. So ordinary it wasn't even noticeable.

It looked like it used to be used for horses; one broken-down side had old stable doors and rickety planks poking outside and rusty nails here and there. I stayed out of there because I wasn't sure if vermin lived in the dusty, hay-filled corners and because it looked like a stiff wind could blow it in. I mostly stuck to the front, which I had made entirely my own over the years. I braided spears of tall prairie grass into necklaces, wore them for a day, then hung them up along the walls. I picked bouquets of the little yellow flowers that grew along the creek—always waiting until they were wilting and about to die—and hung them out to dry. I picked up old nails and bits of rocks and made wind chimes out of them and hung them along the front entrance.

A trail of cottonwoods meandered along the creek and surrounded the barn, making it shady and cool in summer. As I walked along that evening, the seeds snowed down on me as if it were midwinter. Snowing in the early evening sunlight. Water skaters touched down lightly on the creek, making rings grow in the water. Finches sang in the yellow bushes like they were just reborn, which is how I felt when I heard them. Completely alone and surrounded by life at the same time.

I was determined to keep the barn a secret from everyone. The one place in the world that was mine. There was one, big cottonwood that stood up on the ridge, just above the barn. Its giant roots pushed out through the side of the ravine and snaked their way down to the creek. Years ago I had built a dam, just past the tree, to pool the water up around its roots. It made a great swimming hole when the water was high enough. As I got closer to the barn I scanned the sky for its roof. It settled into its place on earth at a slant and sunk into the ground so well it seemed like part of the landscape. I think it used to be red, but it was worn by the weather and was mostly a grayish, old-wood color, with bits of red paint flaking off here and there.

When I saw the crooked roof, I took off at a run. The creek swelled at the pool to waist high. I slipped off my clothes and shoes and plunged into the ice-cold water. When it hit my stomach, I gasped and took a few deep breaths until my skin turned numb and I could stand to float there. I stayed for as long as I could take the ache of the cold, watching the barn swallows dive and turn, catching bugs, letting the gentle current wash the dinner conversation off my body.

I looked down at my feet and legs under the water, they looked like they were melting, stretching and flowing out into the creek. I squinted to try to see them whole, but they were disappearing—into the current and into the land beneath the water. Disappearing into Bourbon County. Suddenly I started gasping for air and scrambled for the bank. I pulled myself up and rubbed my legs hard, back into feeling and warmth. I did my best to wipe the drops of water off my naked body with my hands. As I rubbed my hand across my stomach, I thought of Missy and her protruding belly. I went with her to try on wedding dresses the week before and she left the store in tears, knowing that no dress could cover up a belly that would be seven months and two weeks pregnant on the day of her wedding. I pulled my clothes over my wet, goose-bumped skin and tucked inside the barn.

It smelled like fresh dirt and old hay. I took a deep breath and the walls expanded, then contracted and settled into the dirt a little further. The fiery orange of evening streamed in through cracks in the walls and exposed dust particles dancing.

Missy's folks had kicked her out. She was living with Juan Pablo's family and working in their restaurant. If it weren't for her growing bump I would almost think she was pretending—playing house just like we used to when we were kids.

She was always the bride and she made me be the groom. Missy was persuasive. She picked dandelions and wove them into a tiara for herself. She shoved a pair of socks down my shorts which always caused me to blush, and pushed my hair up under a hat. Now she was making Juan Pablo be the groom. Or maybe her daddy was. JP, he called him. Like if he called him that it would make him less Mexican. All the boys called Juan Pablo, "JP", but ever since Mrs. Mitchell accidentally read his full name out when she was taking attendance, I called him Juan Pablo. I think it's a beautiful name.

The light shafts suddenly disappeared, and the sunlight became thin. I went outside to climb the cottonwood and watch the sunset. Sitting up in that tree I felt like I was part of it all. Part of the growing, green grass. The wind rolling waves across the dreaming sod, part of the sun flashing lightning on the waves. Part of the wet, thawed earth. Part of the giant tree holding me up, reaching its green arms out and up just a little bit further and further every year, trying one day to reach the orange, red sunset. Part of the tremendousness of it all.

I breathed in deep while cottonwood seeds fell over me and rested in my hair and on my bare arms like a blanket. I wished I could dive into the prairie sea. I listened to the wind come from far off across the plain, watched it caress the grass, and then braced for it as it got louder and hit me, blowing more cottony seeds around. Then I saw the most beautiful thing I'd ever seen in my whole life.

The earth itself broke apart and forgot about gravity. At first five or ten then twenty delicate, orange slivers floated up from the ground. Then hundreds of monarch butterflies rose up out of the milkweeds and flew out in all directions. They gathered around the tree, making the cottonwood look alive with orange leaves. They rose and fell with the breeze, part of the air itself, landing on green-gold leaves and brown trunk, turning everything a brilliant, living orange. They were in my hair and all around my face and arms. My breath quickened—I tried not to squeal. I sat perfectly still and let them move all over me. Somewhere between wonder and panic I looked up and saw only a bit of sky that was still a deep blue; everything else was orange. But then the sun dipped low enough into the dusty horizon that the entire sky turned orange too, and I was swallowed up in breathing, moving color. The color of fire.

I held out my arms and the monarchs brushed down, then surged upward again. I floated unbound, their wings, impossibly thin, filling up the air underneath me. Then they swirled and caressed each other, turned north, and flew away. The flames in the sky followed them and the sky turned a pale blue, then almost black. I felt those butterflies even after they vanished, moving inside my stomach and up along my spine. I let them be at home in my skin.

2

WHAT COULD ANYONE THINK OF ME?

At first glance the country is empty, the spaces so wide and barren. You might see a herd of cattle and wonder where the ranch house is. It could be twenty miles away. You might see one lone cow, trying to fit her huge body into the thin shadow made by one lone tree, and wonder where her herd is—and then see no other living thing for miles. But tucked around corners of bluffs and hidden behind bursts of trees are the hidden people of the countryside. They live out here because they want to be left alone. They don't want anyone to tell them how to live. They don't want anyone to tell them nothing. But, inevitably, they need someone. That's when Sandy comes out.

Sandy Topaz was a home care nurse and our friend. She lived in Fort Scott but worked mostly out in the secret places of the county. Sandy came out to visit shut-ins, mentally or physically ill, and elderly folk who no one was looking after or whose loved ones couldn't take care of them anymore.

Because pretty much everyone in that patch of prairie went to Dad's church, especially the elderly ones, we saw Sandy quite a bit. Dad was sometimes the one who called her or convinced someone in the congregation that they should call her. Sometimes Dad even used church money to pay her. And there were times Sandy did the work for free. Dad considered Sandy a partner—she helped sick people with the practical side of things while he took care of the spiritual side. Dad was always working on Sandy to come to church and be baptized, but she was part American Indian and insisted on keeping her own religion.

The day after Sam showed up at our house Sandy came over for dinner. When I had come home after seeing the monarchs the night before, I found Mom standing by the linen closet. The sound of shower water hitting skin drifted into the hallway.

“Mom,” I had whispered, “he's taking a *shower* here?”

“Honey, cleanliness is next to godliness.”

“Sure, but...” I lifted my hands up to show my uncertainty. A thrill brewed in my stomach. She stacked neatly folded sheets into my turned-up hands. “What are you—what, he's *sleeping* here?”

“It was your dad's idea,” she whispered, turning to look down the hall. “Turns out he knows how to fix stuff...build stuff.”

“Who, Dad?”

“Of course not!” Mom looked amused. “No, Sam.”

“So, he's sleeping in our house.”

“Just for a couple days. He's going to build me a fence around the garden. Keep the rabbits out. And he's going to fix the damage the raccoons made in the shed.”

“Why? Do we have money to pay him?”

“In exchange for room and board.”

“Seems like a lot of work just for supper.”

“And breakfast! And lunch! And I'm a good cook, you know.”

“I know. I didn't mean—I just can't believe you're putting a strange boy in the room across the hall.”

Mom looked up at me sort of funny. Then she laid the pillowcases on top of the sheets in my hands.

"He's not a boy, he's a grown up. And he doesn't feel strange, honey." She cocked her head. "I feel like I almost know him already."

The shower had stopped. Mom hurried me into the room we usually reserved for Grandma to put on fresh sheets. I barely slept that night. Before I got into bed I stood at my closed door, fingers on the lock. I pressed my ear against the door to listen for any sound of him, then finally left it unlocked. I was awakened by every train that pulled through. I'd raise my head slightly from the pillow and listen for the sound of Sam's window opening. Or the sound of his door opening. Or the sound of mine.

When Sandy showed up the next evening Sam was working out back, lifting up old railroad ties and hauling them across the yard to use in the garden fence. He had been doing it all day. I watched him out the kitchen window, sweating and grunting under the weight of them. The lace swag framing the window moved slightly with my breath.

"What are you looking at?" Dad asked, making me jump. He was fresh out of the shower and on his way to pray with a family who had just lost their grandpa.

"Just wondering why Mom started hanging the wash out back," I said. "Want me to bring it in?"

"What? Oh no, honey," Mom chirped, "I'll get it. It's warmer in the back just now is all." I'd never known Mom to turn down help with chores, but I watched her go out and take a glass of tea to Sam. She stood with one arm resting on the wash line, watching him toss his head back to get the last drops. He handed the glass back to her and said something that made her bend over with laughter. Sam moved his hand to the wash line too, then pulled it off quickly, probably realizing he was getting rail grease all over the clean towels.

He wiped the sweat from his head with his forearm and smiled. Mom scratched her calf with her foot and tilted her head. I wished I knew what he said that was so funny. "You know, Sandy," Dad said, "Mrs. Baker told me yesterday when I was visiting with her and Joe that you were a godless homewrecker. Says I shouldn't be conversing with you. But if you come on in to worship on Sunday, then we'll save you right there during fellowship."

Sandy could handle my dad better than anyone. Even Mom.

"*Save* me? Now, why would I want that, Reverend? I might lose all my magic." She winked at me. "My people were praying in this country for centuries before you *Presbyterians* showed up," she teased, half in fun and whole in earnest. "Mrs. Baker's just mad because I won't let her feed Joe piles of sugar wrapped in a pie crust."

"Now, Sandy," Dad said, "why don't I tell you the difference between Kansas Reformed Church and Presbyterians."

"No! Good God in Heaven, save me now!" Sandy laughed and threw her arms up to the sky. "Now you see, Reverend, *my* gods would never make us good people sit through a lecture like that."

Dad laughed. "That banana cream pie is the key to the Bakers' forty years of marital bliss," he said.

"I'm sure it is. It's also the key to Joe's diabetes."

I was in awe. If I had said those words, Dad would have skinned me.

Sandy knew how to take the seriousness out of Dad. She handled him just like she did one of her patients. Mom said it was her Indian ways that made her so easy with people from all walks of life. Sandy came from California, and she travelled all across the country, meeting all kinds of people, before she ended up in Kansas.

"I don't care if she never gets baptized," Mom had told Dad

after we first met her. "I know I'll see Sandy in heaven, sitting at the right hand of Jesus."

"Now—"

"Nope! I'll hear nothing of the sort," Mom cut Dad off. Like Mom and Jesus had a secret plan together that they weren't telling anyone.

Mom had cooked up three casseroles, two for the family in grief and one for Sam, Sandy, and us. Dad left, casseroles in hand. Sandy had just come from their house. She was the one who cared for the grandfather, right up until he died.

The plastic on the kitchen chair squeaked as Sandy settled her wide body down on it. Her face was nearly as wide as her body—square shaped, with a strong, straight nose. When she wasn't in her scrubs, she always wore real colorful, long skirts and wide pants, which gave the impression of a giant bouquet of flowers moving toward you when she walked. Sandy might have seemed intimidating, except when you looked into her eyes, she was full of tenderness. They were as black as the moonless sky, her eyes. And they sparkled like that too. She would smile and the corners would crinkle, and you would feel like the stars themselves were winking at you.

I sat down across from her. She sighed and rubbed her temples. Her joyful manner disappeared as soon as Dad left. I felt special that she trusted me with the hard emotions.

"Is it hard," I asked, "to be with someone when they're dying?"

Sandy's eyes sparkled harder as they filled with tears.

"It's an honor," she said, suppressing a cry and nodding her head. "It's an honor." Mom walked by and briefly squeezed her hand. "Sometimes it's harder than others." She took a deep breath.

Sandy knew all about taking in strays. She had about seven or eight stray cats herself. She always had some stray relative sleeping on her couch, too, so she wasn't surprised about Sam sleeping in our house. She swept her long hair behind her shoulders, took another deep breath, and started in, telling Mom and me all the news. We gobbled it up like hungry dogs.

"Did you hear about Bob Lindbergh? Well, he finally found a nice lady—all these years after poor Sherry passed on. She's from *Wichita*, but everyone says she's really nice."

"You don't say! Well, at least she's not from California," Mom winked.

Sandy laughed. "My nephew just left on a road trip from California, heading this way. I can't wait to introduce him to you. He's a good boy. He's got the Medicine, just doesn't know where to put it yet." She wiped the condensation from her tea glass with her shirt sleeve and glanced at me. "You know Bobby Junior? He's gonna be the new fire captain." Bobby Junior was a senior when I was a freshman—and he was already taking over his dad's old job.

"Bless his heart. He's such a good boy."

"I know. I'm so happy he worked out his drinking. His girlfriend, Morgan, was our intern for the past couple years. And now that Bobby's got a steady job, she's finally leaving to go to nursing school. If you ask me, they'll be married by fall." The conversation rose and fell like music, with Sandy pausing at all the right moments for Mom to fill them up with, "Oh my," and "I'll say," and "Bless their hearts!"

"And that leads me to *you,* Jesse," Sandy said.

"Me?" I was rarely involved in the conversation, but I loved to listen. Sandy was one of the only adults who talked without restraint in front of me.

"With Morgan gone, we're in need of a new intern. It doesn't pay much, but it's great work experience. And it might help give you an idea of what you want to do after you graduate."

"You mean, I would learn nursing?" I asked.

"A little bit. I'll do the nursing, you'll fill out the charts, help around the house, that sort of thing. You could come with me on my rounds—keep me company." Sandy looked at me for an answer.

Mom had moved on to dessert and was spooning some rhubarb into a pie crust. She didn't look up, but I could see concern even from the back of her head.

"Well," she said, still spooning the rhubarb, "I don't know what Dad would think of that. He has his heart set on you working with Mrs. Carlson." I looked at Sandy skeptically. Bobby and Morgan were the homecoming king and queen not three years ago. And here they were, already trapped into the rest of their lives. The thought of stepping on that pathway made my stomach turn.

"Then again," Mom sighed, "he's the one who wants you to get a job. Hard work never hurt a soul."

"Oh, we won't make her work too hard," Sandy joked.

"Why don't we talk it over?" Mom stuck the pie in the oven.

"Maybe Jesse could just come with me to one patient," Sandy said. "Try it out and see if everyone is comfortable with the idea. Once a week I see an old friend of mine. Known him for years—very nice guy. Just one patient. Easy as pie." Sandy leaned across the table, grasped my hand, and mouthed the words, *I have a CD player in my car*, and winked.

My eyes widened. This changed everything. "Well, I think it'll be real great," I said.

"*Really* great, honey."

"That'll be really great. Really, it will be," I said. Sandy grinned.

Now, I'm not trying to say that we lived so far out in the country that we didn't even have a CD player. My uncle gave my parents one for Christmas before I was even born. But we only listened to music that was written to praise God or glorify His love. There's some real good stuff that was written for the glory of God, but I just knew Sandy wasn't talking about listening to that kind of music when she whispered that to me;

I just knew Sandy was talking about the kind of music I was not supposed to listen to, the kind that, in my parent's opinion, nobody was supposed to listen to, especially not good people like Sandy. The kind of music that may or may not have been written by the Devil himself. The kind of music I'd been straining to overhear since I found out it existed.

I stood up and floated around the kitchen. My mind was busy picturing Sandy and me rolling up in her Ford Focus, piles of dust billowing out behind the wheels, windows rolled down, and loud music blaring out of the car speakers.

What if Dad was right? What if that music was the instrument of the Devil? A while back, Missy had let me listen to one of her parent's CDs, and I couldn't stop thinking about it for a month straight. I played those songs over and over in my head, trying to not forget what they sounded like. But then, over time, I did forget. I forgot what the music was, but I'll never forget the feeling I got when I heard it. The voices in that music were so different than anything I'd ever heard; it made me feel like I could jump out of my skin and into the singer's. Or like that voice, combined with the drumbeat, were the only things in the world that could *keep* me from jumping out of my skin.

Obviously, I had to get this job. I had to find a way to convince Dad. I formulated a plan while I blindly set the table. Four forks–*I'll wear professional clothes, even if it's hot, or raining, or just fine out, to give the impression of professionalism.* Four knives–*I'll tell him it's God's work to help people.* Four napkins–*even if someone hears us listening to music, it won't matter; we'll be there on business.*

Sam burst through the screen door covered in sweat and rail grease, and I regained my sight. He paused next to Mom.

"I'll just go wash up for dinner," he whispered to her, then brushed past me. "Oh, hey, Jesse."

I caught a brief scent of his sweat and leaned back to watch him walk down the hall. He reached one arm behind his back and peeled off his T-shirt as he ducked into the bathroom. His shirtless back hovered for an instant in the hallway. Four plates—*I am so small. Why am I so excited just to listen to some ordinary music?* My face flushed at my own naiveté. The shower came on. Four glasses—*What could he think of me? What could anyone think of me?*

3

I SAUNTERED

I was deep inside Mom and Dad's closet and the smell of them seeped into my pores. Dad's work shirts were lined up on one side, washed and ironed by Mom every day. She had two shirts ready when it was real hot so he could change halfway through the day into a nice, clean one. Mom's clothes were hung, grouped by color, on the other side. Mostly they were blue—jeans and church dresses.

I was raiding her clothes to see if I could find something other than cutoff jean shorts and my cousin's hand-me-down T-shirts to wear to work with Sandy, still hoping if Dad saw me all dressed up, he might let me take the internship.

I had just picked up Mom's only pair of real leather shoes and smelled the old, earthy scent when I heard the floor creak. I peeked out the open side of the sliding door. Sam stood there, staring at the room. I froze, clutching the shoe and wondering if he was looking for something to steal before taking off. Then I scolded myself for letting the Devil enter my mind and accuse the innocent.

He took in a deep breath, then looked around at the bed, the dresser, and Mom's jewelry box—but he didn't touch anything, just looked. So I looked at him. He was still wearing the same tight, army-green peace sign T-shirt, but Mom had washed it and he looked clean.

It started getting hot in the closet. Like the scorching east wind blowing down on the head of Jonah hot. Sweat beaded around my eyes and temples and trickled down the sides of my face. I didn't dare move to wipe it and give it away that I was watching him, so I sat there perfectly still and let it tickle my neck.

Sam moved with the timidity of a bird; he barely made a wake in the air around him. Sweat dripped down from my neck, heading for the vee of my T-shirt. I opened my mouth to breathe silently, hoping he would leave before I couldn't stand it anymore and had to burst out the closet door for a gulp of fresh air. Sam ran his hand along the bedspread, brought it up to his nose and sniffed it. He took in the smell, sat on the bed, and then sort of let his head fall into his hands. I thought maybe he was crying. But then he shook his head, stood up and walked out. That was it. I raised my shirt and wiped the sweat off my face.

I sat quiet for a while, hoping he would come back and hoping he wouldn't. Then I grabbed a white blouse with white embroidered flowers on it, a khaki skirt, and the other leather shoe and skipped out of there.

Another night passed with Sam still sleeping in our house. A couple days had turned into four, each day with Sam getting up real early to start working in the yard. I woke to the sound of him banging on wood or hauling dirt around in the wheelbarrow. He had to get started early because part of the day would be lost to the heat. Sometimes, I would peek out the curtains in my room and see him just sitting there, staring off into the distance or eyeing rollie pollies in the dirt. Other times, Mom would be out there with him, holding the wood steady while he sawed it, or just keeping him company while he dug post trenches. He had a little black notebook with a pen attached to it that he wrote in sometimes. Maybe those were the times when he was talking to God like he said out there on the lobster boat.

As soon as Sam started mending the fence around the garden, I volunteered to pull dandelions with unusual fervor. Dad assumed I had listened to his words about being less wild and congratulated himself for it.

"Directing the choir in the nice, air-conditioned church will sound pretty good after you do some manual labor. Kind of like when Mom moved out here with me and left the farm."

Mom was slightly bewildered, but she seemed too distracted by Sam's presence to really care.

"They'll go to seed if I don't get them now," I told her. "Just saving myself more work later."

"I've never known you to think ahead," she said with a smile. "I guess you're growing up. Help me carry this timber out for Sam, will you? He's as hardworking as an ant at harvest. We sure are lucky he hopped off that train."

There were about a million dandelions in the tiny garden, so I figured if I took a lot of care to dig deep and get the roots, I could plan it to take just about as much time as it would take Sam to fix the fence. We didn't talk much. He sawed and sanded and drilled and hammered. Every so often he would gaze up at the endless Kansas sky, then pull the notebook out of his back pocket and write something down. I hummed to keep myself from saying something stupid. Once, when I was hauling a bag of dandelions to the side of the house, he talked to me.

"It's a shame you're wasting all those."

"What do you mean?" I asked. "They're just weeds."

"I read you can make wine out of them," he said. "Almost as good as making it from water, huh?"

Another time when he was writing in his notebook, he

looked up at me and watched me pulling. I felt those green eyes. I always knew what direction they were looking.

"You like it here, right?" he asked. "I mean, like what your dad said—you like running around all over the..." he trailed off and gestured out behind the house.

"Sure," I shrugged. "I like the wilderness."

He laughed. "This isn't wilderness."

"It's not?"

"I mean—Jesse, you should see a rainforest, or the mountains, or...do you ever want to leave?"

"Are you kidding?" I blurted. "Of course I want to leave. You think I don't want to see a rainforest?"

He nodded and went back to writing. "That's what I thought," he said. Just then a train come rumbling through. "Have you ever thought about jumping on one of the trains?"

My heart practically jumped out of my body and hopped onboard the one right there. He didn't even look up from his notebook.

"No," I breathed. "Yes," I gulped. "I mean—maybe. Just—not on my own."

He smiled with his picket fence teeth. "Oh, you mean you want someone to go with you?"

Words couldn't get past the heart in my throat which had recently jumped up into higher regions, so I just nodded. He nodded back at me and wrote something down. When my throat had stopped beating and I could speak again, I summoned my courage.

"Have you thought about," I mumbled, "—do you know when you're gonna hop back on?"

"Ah, well. You know the train schedule better than me, Jesse," he said, and went back to hammering.

That evening Sam came in the house humming. It was funny because Mom had been humming all day and somehow, even though I'm sure Sam wasn't humming a hymn like Mom, their melodies seemed to match. I was lying on the floor in front of the record player in the living room, listening to music and reading album covers. I liked to isolate the parts of the orchestra in my head: the brass, the high strings, the low strings, the woodwinds, and especially if it had a choir, the voices.

Mom was already in the kitchen humming, and when Sam swung the back door open his song and Mom's seemed to circle round one another, like a flute and a trumpet. Then the songs played and shook and curled up and harmonized. I heard Mom laugh and lifted my chin from my forearm to glance that direction. Mom was hidden behind the open pantry door, and I could just see Sam, grinning.

He grabbed Mom's hand and pulled it out into view and up above his head, then circled round behind the pantry door as well. Suddenly Mom came twirling out into the open, hair flying all around her, and a grin as wide as the red sea. She almost whirled into the table, but Sam grabbed her hand fast, pulled her toward him, hand on her hip and spun her back toward the pantry.

I raised up on my elbows, eyes wide, neck craning to see around the pantry door. The music from the record quieted to a whisper. For a full minute the kitchen was as still as pre-dawn. Then Mom cleared her throat. "Well," she said.

"I better go shower," Sam said, his voice warm and full like a contrabass.

Jesus turned water into wine and all the people drank it and were awed by the miracle. Psalms says we are meant to praise God with trumpet, harp, lyre, strings and pipe, and clash of symbols. And *dance.*

But just how alcohol can lead to debauchery, drunkenness, and carousing; dancing can lead to lustful flesh. We must endeavor to be made full by the Holy Spirit, not by drink or lust. Well, that's how Dad explains it anyway.

When Sam strode past the living room and down the hall, he didn't notice me lying there. But I was filled with something. Something vivid and colossal and strange and I don't dare even utter holy. My spirit was made full with a longing as big as the world.

Mom needlessly swept over the kitchen counter with a cloth and stepped out the door onto the back porch. I watched her flushed face through the window as she smoothed her hair and gazed at the cloudless sky. One solo violin etched its bow across one lonely string, and the song ended.

That night at dinner Sam seemed to be in a particularly good mood. Mom made seven-layer Mexican casserole and even put on one of her Wednesday night Bible study dresses. Dad entertained us with stories about the leaky church basement, which he was personally patching up after the previous minister had been treacherously cheated by the mason.

"I called the same company to come fix it, but they claimed it had passed the allotted time of the guarantee. I'll tell you, these people feel perfectly fine cheating a *church*. If I had been here when the work was ordered I would have hired a local company—not some fly-by-night business out of Wichita, set on cheating people with false guarantees. It's a rip off. They think because I'm a minister I'm not going to know their scam, but I know. I know. Just like those air-vac guys..." Dad had a way of going on and on about falsehoods and scams. It's on account of his cleverness we weren't cheated out of house and home every day. I guess when money was as scarce as it was for us, you couldn't be too careful.

"I'm sure they meant well," Mom said. "Folks are just trying to make a living. Even in Wichita." Sometimes I wonder what would come of Dad without Mom's supervision.

"I know what you mean," Sam spoke up. "My dad doesn't really give a—a care about anyone other than himself. He'd cheat all of Portland and not even notice he was doing it."

"Oh?" Dad raised his eyebrows. "What do your parents do for a living, Sam?"

"My dad's a lawyer," Sam said. "And my mom is an architect." Dad nearly choked on all seven layers and Mom's eyes got real wide. "Typical authoritarian father," he glanced at me, "you know."

Sam volunteered to do the dishes after dinner, and I jumped to help. We stood, arm to arm, at the sink. He washed and I dried and put away while Dad sat in the living room working on Sunday's sermon and Mom put new sheets on all the beds.

"What do you want to do after you graduate?" Sam asked.

"Oh, um," I glanced behind me, "I don't know. I guess—well, I want to see the ocean," I whispered. "I don't even care which one, but—we can't afford it. I'll probably just end up in Fort Scott."

"Jesse," Sam chuckled. He leaned toward me. "You don't have to do what your dad says. You know that, right?"

"But—" I stammered, "but—how?"

"There's always a way," he said. "Trust me."

The eighth night Sam stayed with us was the night the heat broke through the last gates of spring and clung to us, settling in for the rest of the summer. Apparently, the garden fence was taking longer than Sam thought, and no one talked about him leaving anymore. Mom hummed around the house all day, when she wasn't laughing from something clever Sam said to her. She acted like he ought to just move in for good.

When you do nothing but pull weeds all day, you start to see them on the inside of your eyelids. I laid in bed that night with dandelions and Sam's neck, his jaw, his green eyes—splashing across my vision, wondering how I would get any sleep the entire summer if it stayed this hot. The cotton tank top I slept in was sticking to my back with sweat. I kicked all the covers off, even the pillows, so that the bed was bare. I don't quite know how I knew it, but I became aware that Sam was sitting outside my window. He had an energy in him that spread out around him, touching everything nearby, wherever he went. I felt it the afternoon when he first walked up to the porch. And I felt it that night lying in bed.

I felt him sitting out on the old railroad ties he'd piled up near my window that morning, leaning his back against the house. I felt the heat from him come through the wall, spread out over my sheets and into the springs of the mattress. It was too hot.

He was probably out there studying the cicadas.

"What kind of crickets do you have out here?" he had asked the first night he stayed with us.

"Those aren't crickets," Mom had laughed. "They're cicadas."

"They're louder than the freight train," Sam had joked.

But he was right. They were the seventeen-year cicadas. They were smaller than regular ones but ten times as loud. And there were more of them covering the tree trunks in the evenings than even Mom or Dad could remember. Cicadas bury themselves in the dirt right after they're born, then emerge a year or two later metamorphosed. They crawl out of their hard, rattly shells with giant, translucent wings, shimmering blue, looking like angels just dug up from the center of the earth. And the seventeen-year ones spent seventeen whole years down in the darkness, becoming who they're meant to be. Then after one sacrosanct summer-long song they lay their eggs and die. Some nights the cicadas started singing and you couldn't hear yourself talk. Sam thought it sounded like an alarm—he couldn't sleep—but to me it was a lullaby.

"Which ones make so much noise?" Sam had asked when we were in the garden. "The ones getting ready to die? Or the ones who just came out of the ground?"

"The new ones, of course," I had said. "You only sing like that when you've just realized you're something glorious."

Sam's heat was getting to be too much, so I slid down to the end of the bed and opened the window. I figured he would hear it—but the cicadas were so loud I don't think he did. At any rate he didn't move. I turned around and laid my head at the foot of the bed by the open window, hoping to get a breeze. Instead of wind, the cicada buzz flowed through in waves, crashing against the thick air.

Fireflies twirled around the trees, and when I looked at the horizon and squinted, it looked like the sky stretched all the way to my house and the stars were dancing. I wondered if it was okay for stars to do it. I shifted, giving my back and stomach turns at burning. I pushed my hands against the wall, imagining only a thin layer of wood separating them from Sam's back. *Why won't he come in?* I thought. *Why won't he let me cool down? Why won't he come inside and glide past his own bedroom door and enter my room? I shouldn't think like that. I shouldn't want things so much. But I can't sleep, I'll* never *be able to sleep, unless...*

I let my mind wander, and my hands wander, and the room sweltered and dampened until, at some point, Sam must've gotten up and headed in because it cooled down and the cicada song brought me to sleep.

The next morning, I tried to cool down in the shower, but the heat was bossy. It shoved into my skin the moment the water turned off. Mom must have felt it too because she looked flushed and tired. Dad had been gone until real late the night before, and she said she didn't sleep much. Even Sam looked like the heat was keeping him up all night. Mom was so hot she didn't eat breakfast with me, preferring a shower to a piece of toast. I felt a flash of shame, wondering if she somehow knew my thoughts, if she somehow knew what I had felt the night before.

"This house is filthy," she announced when she got out of the shower.

I glanced around and blinked—the house was as clean as it always was.

"I need to scrub this floor without you two tracking dirt in," she said. "Jesse, why don't you take Sam to Fort Scott and pick up some corn on the cob for supper?"

My heart beat faster.

"You sure?" Sam asked. He rose from the table and joined Mom at the sink. "I can stay—I mean—I can be clean."

"No. I'm sure," Mom said, barely glancing at him while she took his plate from his hands and washed it.

Dad had started driving the church van into work because it had air conditioning. That left us with the Brown Bomber.

Sam and I walked out to the mud-colored Buick and I went around to the driver's side and opened the door. He looked at me kind of funny.

"You know how to drive?" he asked.

"Yeah."

"Aren't you a bit young to be driving?"

"Well, in Kansas you can get your license when you're fourteen so you can help out on the farm," I explained.

"But you don't live on a farm," he said.

"Yeah, but the law is for the whole state. So even kids in the city can drive at fourteen." He just looked at me. "Anyway, I've been driving for almost two years already. I can drive—just get in," I said, trying to sound cool.

"Okay." He sounded hesitant, but he got in the passenger seat. "Man, this is scarier than hopping a freight car," he joked, but he did look scared.

I couldn't help but laugh. I was trying to be tough, but suddenly I got all giggly. I sat down and the upholstery burned the bare part under my knees. I rolled the window down and breathed out.

"Now, where are you taking me?" he asked.

I was going to tell him just to the store, like Mom said, but then I looked at him out of the corner of my eye and got an idea.

"Wanna drive out to the Flint Hills?" I asked.

"The what hills?"

"The Flint Hills. It's a real pretty area, to the north. There's a river, a couple lakes. We can hit the store on the way back. Anyway, you could see part of the state that way."

He smiled real big. "I'd love that," he said.

We headed down our dirt road and out to the old highway. We were rolling along pretty good, and Sam seemed happy to be out on the road again. The wind and sun touched his face, and he rested his head back on the seat to take in the countryside.

"This is nice," I said, "to see you in your element."

He started up, like I'd found him out when he was hiding.

"Hmm, you're not everything you appear at first sight, are you?" he said looking at me.

"I hope not," I said, though I wasn't quite sure what I meant by it. The wind whipped my hair into my face, so I pulled my knee up to steer and put my hair back in a ponytail.

"Man, you *can* drive!" he said. Then he let out a big, "Woohoo!" and stuck his arms out the window to let the wind stroke them.

I pulled my sunglasses on and pushed my foot down harder on the gas. There were few things in life I loved more than a good, long drive. Something about the vastness of the plains made me feel so calm, like knowing how small I was made life easier to handle. The prairie opened up in front of us like a big, wide sea. The Flint Hills off to the north looked like islands with trees winding around them, lining the water. Cattle and horses were scattered here and there, searching for shade. A grain silo rose in the distance like a lighthouse. A different hawk sat watchful on nearly every telephone pole. We passed a giant, faded billboard that read: *Without a Shadow of a Doubt: Jesus is Alive.* The land rose and fell all around us, and we floated through it. The deep heat had turned the green deep; the newness of the color was gone. Sky touched prairie in every direction. Crests of wild daisies broke along the highway, and in front of us was just the road. The longest thing I could imagine.

"If we kept driving," I said, "we would end up in California."

Sam nodded slowly, like he knew what I meant, *really*. Then he looked at me. It gave me goosebumps on that hot day.

"It feels like freedom, doesn't it?" he asked, still looking. "You know, Jesse, the train goes all the way to the ocean, too." I nearly fainted. He reached his arms up behind his head. "All the way to the big blue, baby."

I bent down and turned the tape deck on to keep from hyperventilating. The sound of the wind rushed past our ears, so I turned it up loud.

After a few minutes Sam shouted over the wind. "I know this one, I think."

"It's Debussy, 'Claire de Lune.'"

"Oh, right! That's why I know it—I remember my high school music teacher told us a story about how he was the rock star of his time. Had an affair with some Parisian lady."

"Really?"

"Yeah—that's the only reason I remember it," he said.

"But the music—it's so beautiful," I said, frowning.

Sam laughed. "Your dad's a trip, man," he said, moving his arm out the window like a wave. "Like he can keep the bad stuff out of life. It's not separated. I mean, sex and drugs and God and rock music and dancing and beauty and swearing. It's all humanity. It's not one or the other. It's all mushed up together."

I didn't say a word—I couldn't; I was too busy trying to picture God's love being mushed up with rock music, dancing, swearing, and sex. And trying to be calm about how Sam could talk about sex and drugs as if he was talking about the weather. We spent the next half hour listening to the tape, the wind and sun beating against our reddening arms.

Sam finally spoke. "How did you end up being a high school senior if you're only fifteen?"

"Mom and Dad wanted me to read the Bible, so Mom taught me how to read when I was really young." I thought about it for a minute. "She taught me to read, then gave me this giant book full of violence and..." I couldn't say the word *sex* in front of him. "Have you ever read the Old Testament?"

Sam shook his head.

"Well. I was good at reading, so I skipped kindergarten. Our school is small, and first and second grades were in one class, so I kind of just ended up in second grade at age five."

"Your mom taught you, huh?" Sam asked. I nodded. "She's pretty smart. Did she ever read anything else to you?"

I shook my head. "Nope. Just the Bible. But I've read other books in school," I hastened to add.

"Your parents were okay with that?" he asked.

"There were a couple they didn't let me read. I got a special exemption on account of religious objections. But mostly they thought since I had a good foundation with the Bible, I could interpret other books in a Christian like manner."

"That's why you go outside all day," he said.

I shrugged, not really knowing what he meant.

I decided to take Sam to my favorite place in the Flint Hills, a small lake tucked inside the shade of the bur oaks, a little bit out of the way. We pulled off the highway and turned down a dirt road. The rush of wind quieted, and bird song drifted into the open windows. Sam's smile widened. I hoped he would like the spot I'd picked.

Tree shadows passed, making it look like a giant spotlight flashing on and off, casting strange shapes over our bodies. I imagined it was what the ocean floor looked like in shallow water. Distracted by the shadows, the tide would pull us deeper into the sea. We reached the lake and stopped, letting the dust settle, then got out of the car. Silence fell on us. My body felt like it was still moving out in front of me.

"This is really pretty," Sam said, sounding surprised.

"Yeah." I wished I could think of something smarter to say.

Sam looked at it for a long minute, then started down to the shore. "You coming?" he called behind him.

We scrambled down the little hill and were both sweating like crazy by the time we got to the water. Without the wind from the moving car, the heat was oppressive.

"Is it safe to swim here?" Sam asked.

"Sure, why not? What do you think—there's gonna be sharks?" I tried a joke.

"Let's get in." He stooped and started unlacing his shoes.

He began to undress in the bold sunlight right in front of me, and I thought I might have a panic attack.

"I didn't bring my swimsuit!" I blurted. "We can't swim. We don't have our suits."

He looked up at me, socks coming off. "Jesse, it's like, a hundred degrees out here—hotter even." He looked around. "There's nobody here but us, and I'm getting in."

With that he reached one arm up behind his neck and pulled off his T-shirt. I felt dizzy. I almost couldn't breathe, or I was breathing too much, I don't know. He had muscles right above his jeans—I'd never seen a body like that before.

"Oh my God," I said under my breath and bit my lip. I didn't know if I was swearing or praying. Sam looked up and stopped undressing, just before he slipped his jeans off.

"We don't have to go *skinny dipping*, Jesse," he said with

a grin. "Just a swim. C'mon, you can leave your underwear on. It will dry in five minutes in this heat. The drive back will be more bearable."

Then he *did* slip off his jeans and started running straight for the water, with just his underpants on.

"C'mon, Jesse!" he hollered back at me, "I won't look–I promise!"

That image is burned in my memory forever.

Now, this was one of those times when you can see your life playing out in front of you like a movie. *Okay,* I thought, *I can do this. Underpants and bra are the same as a bikini, just like Missy wears.* I looked under my shirt to remember which bra I was wearing that day–purple. I remembered we bought it because it was on sale at Walmart. *It's completely fine; no one will ever know. He promised not to look, we'll be dry in five minutes, and if I don't do this right now, I will regret it for the rest of my life.*

I stepped out of my flip flops. I pulled off my sweaty shirt and took a deep breath. Then I slipped my shorts off and–I didn't even run–I sauntered down toward the water.

First, I felt the sun on my bare skin, then a faint, whisper of a breeze, then the feel of those green eyes on parts of me they'd never touched before, then the ecstasy of the cool water.

"I thought you promised not to look," I said.

"Sorry," he looked embarrassed and put his chin in the water, "I meant not to," he said.

Then I disappeared under the water.

4

ELECTRICITY

From that day on the rest of the summer was as hot as Job's bones. It sucked the moisture out of crops and blew a deathly, searing breath on the weak cattle. Sandy got real worried about elderly folk dying of heat stroke. When your life depends on the land, you get preoccupied with the weather. The drought was all anyone could talk about, and Dad had to start giving sermons on it.

"For the sun is no sooner risen with a burning heat, but it withereth the grass," the Bible says, *"and the flower thereof falleth, and the grace of the fashion of it perisheth: so also shall the rich man fade away in his ways.* Therefore let us not judge God's ways, but instead, seek the wisdom given to us through these hard times. Now let us pray for rain."

Dad managed to keep the pews packed full and the congregation singing with a tone not heard in Bourbon County for years. Dad said the drought scared them into church to pray for rain, but I knew the real reason for Bourbon County's enthusiastic devotion: air conditioning.

It was the drought that drove them into church alright, but it wasn't to pray. Cool air blasted out of floor vents at the ends of every other pew. Parishioners fought over who would get to sit next to them. Mrs. Schumer came a half hour early every Sunday and positioned her plump body in such a way to allow her skirt to cover the vent and the air to blow up into it, filling it up like a sail and blocking the air for everyone else. People glared at her, but she just sat there, fanning herself with the program, skirt poofed out like a Victorian lady.

The drought had gotten mean. It punched your body every time you walked outside. So, the beaten congregation took to staying as long as possible after the service. Everyone had a question for Dad or something they wanted to pray about.

Dad ate it up. I wondered if he was secretly praying for the drought to continue. His flock was at his feet, scrambling to be led—and to drink Mom's sun tea.

Down in the fellowship hall, in the basement, it felt like a walk-in refrigerator. Dad meandered through the flock giving out knowledge while they all worked themselves up sharing anecdotes about crops dying and livestock dying and old people dying. To Mrs. Schumer he said, "I know your grandson believes this is from the climate change—let me ask you this: are we greater than God? Are we humble humans capable of changing God's own creation, spoiling His own desires? It seems to me a type of arrogance to believe we are more capable than God. This planet is in His hands. And the best thing we can do is pray."

And to Mr. Richardson, "Now we must remember, just because we pray for rain doesn't mean we're going to get it. God does not grant us every prayer we utter. Imagine if He did! What chaos would reign on this Earth? God will grant us the relief we seek, only if He deems it best. We must remember that we are held in His love. If rain doesn't come, it is because God wants the drought for us. We cannot begin to grasp His ways."

Our house, insulated as well as could be from the heat, was a dark oven. We didn't have air conditioning, so Mom closed the windows and curtains the minute the sun rose and opened all the windows at nightfall. Sam had been in our house for two weeks, and I had finally gotten used to running into him in the hallway.

Ever since our drive—well, our swim—I felt excitement coming through me. Like it was *me* that was stirring everything up around me. Dad was so busy with all the extra praying and counseling, he agreed to let me go to work with Sandy without much persuasion.

I felt electric driving to meet Sandy. I wore the clothes from Mom's closet: a khaki, knee-length, linen skirt; a white, button-down, short-sleeve blouse with white, embroidered flowers; and the leather flats.

"Well don't you look nice!" Sandy said. "You didn't have to dress up."

I shrugged my shoulders and acted like it was nothing.

"Now, Jesse," Sandy said sternly as I climbed into her Ford, "I know that you have the prettiest singing voice in the county, and I consider it my civic duty to introduce you to some music I know you've never heard before. If I were you, I'd think about using that voice of yours to get a scholarship."

I furrowed my brow. "How do you know if I can sing or not?"

"Everyone knows you can sing! Word spreads in Bourbon County."

"But I only ever sing in church."

"You know how it is here—if you don't want something printed on the front page of the newspaper, don't do it," she said with a laugh. "Here." She slipped a CD into the stereo.

"What is it?"

"I made a mix CD for you. I know it's old-fashioned, but that's what we did when I was your age. I hope you like it."

"Sandy," I said, "aren't you a little afraid that if Dad finds out he'll tar and feather you?"

"Well," she laughed, "I know your parents don't agree with this type of music, but I think I picked songs that they would approve of."

That was disappointing.

"I might still be run out on a rail for subversion," she smiled, "but I consider your education worth the risk."

"Thank you," I said. "What's subversion?"

"Oh, that means...well, to undermine someone else's principles. To overthrow...to *corrupt*," she winked.

I leaned back and let the air conditioning dry out my sweaty blouse. The highway flew by much faster with the windows rolled up. I gazed out at the passing power lines and waited, with a fluttering in my stomach, for the music to begin. It was soft and slow at first. Sound swelled up around me like the lake water. Not rushing, just...seeping. One piano, one lonely voice. An untrained voice. The genuine, aching, thumping, scratching, weeping voice of the human heart. The most real sound. It covered me, and I sunk beneath it.

Sandy didn't speak for the first several songs and I almost forgot she was there—and I was there—and we were riding in a car. Finally, she broke the silence.

"Did you know that ancient people didn't have a word for the color blue? I just read that the other day. Scientists think that people actually couldn't see the color because they didn't have a name for it. Isn't that amazing?" She was looking up at the cloudless sky, not quite yet scorching.

"But the sky and the water...aren't they the most obvious things?" I asked.

"Well, that's what we think," Sandy said. "But I wonder what we can't see yet—because we don't have a name for it."

Electric guitars and deep drumbeats spread around the Ford and pulsed my blood as we moved down the highway toward the Missouri border.

My heartbeat sped up or slowed down in rhythm with the

music. My skin tingled, my muscles oscillated between rest and movement—almost dance movement—as if I had no choice in the matter. *This is it,* I thought. *This is what Dad calls the Devil. Something as untouchable as sound is controlling my body.*

But then, Mozart or Beethoven—my body reacts to hearing them too. Just in a different way. Why are these songs so bad? They were written with intention, just like the others. Instruments are vessels; it is the intention of the player that matters. How do we know the music Sandy was playing wasn't written to glorify God? New thoughts, hidden in folds of sound, snuck into my mind. Maybe God's glory comes in different forms, like even in the form of being in love with another human. Maybe even that love, sinful love, is worth singing about.

"*It was not you who sent me here, but God,*" I said out loud.

"What's that, sweetie?" Sandy asked.

"Joseph. The one with the coat," I said. Sandy raised her eyebrows.

I closed my eyes and listened some more. Thoughts flew past my eyelids like the fence posts flashing by on the side of the highway. Plans, intention, love, sin—it might have been the Devil working hard and fast through the reverberations of the sound waves crashing against me, but I resolved right then and there in Sandy's Ford that songs inspired by romantic love or even heartache were just as holy as those inspired by God's love. A sense of understanding washed over me. I may not have known what it felt like to make love, but I knew what love sounded like.

Trees moved in around us and the road began to tilt upward and downward in mellow hills. We drove past the ranchland and turned down where the plateau dropped off and the trees come up in a dense forest.

"Have you ever been swimming up in the Flint Hills?" I asked Sandy.

"Oh, I love it up there, but you're not going to get me in a swimsuit!" she said. "Why—you already thinking about skipping out on work and going swimming instead?" she teased.

"Oh, no! I'm real happy to be here with you," I said. "I was just thinking about it."

"Mmmhmm," Sandy responded.

"Have you ever been in love?" I asked, the music making me bold.

"Well! *There's* a question!" Sandy was happy now; this was much juicier than talking about the Flint Hills. "Of course I've been in love!" she almost shouted. "I can't even count how many times I've been in love! I'm in love right now!" I had to laugh. "The question is, sweetie, have *you*?"

"*Me?*" I blurted out, trying to sound shocked. "I don't know about me, I mean, who would I even—I don't know," I stumbled. "I was just hoping you would tell me about the first time you knew you were in love. I mean when you for sure knew."

"Okay, well, that one isn't so exciting." She looked down at her hands on the steering wheel and was quiet for a minute. "I was in high school," she said finally. "The really interesting love story is the one that led me to Kansas."

"You came out to Kansas because you were in love?"

"Oh, yes. Well, in a roundabout sort of way. You wanna hear the story?"

"Definitely."

"I was in college at Stanford. It's an expensive school, but I had scholarships. My mom didn't want me to go. She wanted me to stay home so I could keep taking care of her, my mom was—is—not well. But I was determined. I really wanted to go to the big city, to see different kinds of people. I knew I was smarter than she thought I was. I knew I could make it with the smart kids—like you, Jesse.

"So I worked hard, got scholarships, and when I got there

I met new people, and they all sort of collectively blew my mind. I'd never felt like that before—I was in my element for the first time. I was in love with all of them, really, because I was in love with the person *I* was when I was with them. The person I was becoming."

Sandy's voice was lively and loud. She laughed as she talked, she shouted sometimes. It was such a shift from the stillness of my house. Her hands moved around, and she switched them off and on the steering wheel.

"There was this one in particular though, Quinn, who I deeply, truly loved with all my heart and soul," Sandy went on.

"How did you know it?" I interrupted. "How did you know you loved Quinn like that?"

"Hmm, that's a tough one...I think I knew that the world would never be the same. It was like I got on board a different earth, in a different universe. It looked the same, but it felt different. I knew that life was better, profoundly better, because of that love. Even if Quinn and I didn't end up together, life would always be better because I knew that love existed. Does that make sense?"

"I don't know," I said truthfully. "But how did Quinn get you to move to Kansas from California? Why would you leave such a cool place to come out here?"

Sandy laughed. "Well, I think Kansas can be cool, too. But here's the story: Quinn, along with some of our other friends, was in a band. A *rock* band." She glanced over at me, half smiling. My eyes widened.

"They were getting ready to take this old, beat-up van on tour for the summer. And I really wanted to come along—I couldn't imagine being separated for the whole summer—but girlfriends weren't allowed. Band members only. It was a strict rule, understandably, since girlfriends or boyfriends of band members always mess up the band—look at Yoko! Look at Fleetwood Mac!"

I had no idea what she was talking about, but I didn't let on.

"Well, Quinn," she sighed, "felt the same as me. We just couldn't bear to be apart all summer long. So, I joined the band."

"I didn't know you played an instrument," I said.

"Well, I don't! Or let me rephrase: I didn't. But by the time we reached L.A. from San Francisco, I was the best tambourine player on the West Coast. I was tambourine shaker and part time back-up singer. Quinn was the lead singer," she sighed through a goofy grin.

"We headed east at L.A. and played at any podunk little town where we could get a gig. Especially if they fed us or gave us money. We played in Las Vegas at the most run-down hotel off the strip, we played in the seediest bars I've ever seen smack dab in the middle of Mormon country in Utah. Then we hit those Rocky Mountains." Sandy's sparkly eyes sparkled even harder. She never talked like this at our dinner table.

"My God, that giant wall of mountains was like nothing I'd ever seen. I didn't think we could make it over them. I thought we'd be stuck in Western Colorado forever. I remembered this story about the pioneers coming west—it was a story from my grandpa on my mom's side, the white side.

"When the pioneers got to the Rocky Mountains, after they'd been traveling for months and months on those Conestoga wagons, through blizzard and drought and famine, leaving every comfort they had ever had, they saw the Rockies in the distance, and they thought they were close. But they traveled for days and days more, and all the while the Rockies were getting bigger and closer. But they were still so far away. And when they finally got up close to them and fully understood the terrible majesty and the sheer greatness of their size, they climbed down out of their wagons, and they wept. They just wept."

Sandy paused and looked out in the distance, seeing the mountain range in her mind's eye. I looked ahead too, trying to imagine what a mountain would look like in person.

"I always loved that story," Sandy went on more quietly, "because I imagined it was the Rocky Mountains that kept the settlers from reaching California and murdering all the Indians there, at least for a few more years. To see them in person, well, it was just incredible."

Sandy slowed down a bit and glanced up at the cypresses.

"Well," she sighed, "we drove that old van right through the magnificent Rockies. I thought, *how ironic that now we can just drive through*. We'd been on tour for a couple weeks then, and Quinn and I started getting on each other's nerves. It was a tight space—nowhere to be alone. The other band members were sick of hearing us fight. They regretted letting me join the band. It was getting pretty tense when fate stepped in to save us. The van—that old thing that was held together with duct tape, it finally broke down for good. In Wichita."

"No way."

"Yep. We were all flat broke. No one could afford to repair the van. We played as many gigs as we could in the area, but it wasn't enough money to get us out of there. We were stuck. The drummer knew there was no way he could get his drum set back without the van, so he sold it at a pawn shop and used the money to buy a ticket home. The others, including Quinn, called their parents and got airline tickets back to San Francisco. I knew my mom couldn't afford it, so I had to get a job."

"No *way*!"

"Yep. There I was in Wichita, Kansas, the love of my young life had just abandoned me and flown back to California, and I was homeless and unemployed. I thought I'd get a job for a couple weeks—long enough to save enough money for a bus ticket—and then get back to San Francisco in time for classes to begin in the fall. I had to sleep at the homeless shelter."

"Weren't you sad—about Quinn leaving you like that?"

"Of course—devastated. And hungry. But here's what I learned, Jesse. Things beyond basic survival only have power in our lives if we choose to let them have power. Eventually, the hunger took over."

"Why did you stay?" I asked in shock. "Why would anyone from California decide to stay in Wichita?"

"The Keeper of the Plains," Sandy said.

"What, the statue?"

"The very one."

I'd seen the statue before on a school trip to Wichita. We drove past it on our way to the history museum there. I could hardly think of why that would persuade Sandy to stay in Kansas.

"I got a job waiting tables at a Mexican-Irish restaurant," Sandy went on. "I was a good waitress because I was used to waiting on my mother. Although mostly I just cried into people's margaritas—I missed Quinn and the band so much," she laughed. "But one night after work I was walking along the river there—the Arkansas River—and I saw it: the Keeper of the Plains, standing out in the middle of the river, at the union of the Arkansas with the Little Arkansas." Sandy reached one arm out and held her palm to the sky. "His arms stretched out so high, his head raised to the Great Spirit. He doesn't look like my Indians. I mean, he's a Plains Indian," she put her hand back on the wheel. "But he was so beautiful. The river was high that year. Water rushed down all around him, but he didn't falter. I stood on the bank, transfixed. Then, right at that moment, giant flames shot up all around him. It was one of the most incredible things I've ever seen. They light him up at sunset. I didn't know. I took it as a sign. He was looking out for the plains, keeping watch, but in that moment, I felt like he was looking out for me too. For the first time in my life someone was keeping watch over *me*. And so I stayed. Because of the Keeper of the Plains."

I was stunned into silence.

Sandy slowed down and we turned up a dusty road that was lined with cottonwoods and cypress trees. The sun was burning my arm through the window, so I positioned the air vent to blow right on it, thinking of the statue, imagining it circled with fire.

Sandy told me we were checking in on an elderly man named Billy. She called him Mr. Billy. She said he suffered from self-neglect. He was socially isolated, living way out up in the woods like he did, but he was too stubborn to move into town and into the nursing home like he should.

"It's not really part of the job to check up on him as much as I do," Sandy explained, "but I like him."

We reached a clearing in the woods and pulled up to a rundown-looking mobile home. Sandy left her purse and the tablet where I was supposed to put in patient information on the back seat and opened the car door. The heat hit us like a brick wall.

There was no car and no sign of life, really. A pile of chopped wood was stacked up outside against the wall, but it looked like it'd been there for decades, covered in moss and spiderwebs. There were some random tools lying around—a shovel, a hammer, and a box of rusted nails. Nothing looked like it got used at all. Sandy knocked real loud on the door.

"You have to talk loudly, otherwise he won't be able to hear you," she said. Then she cracked open the door. It was unlocked. "Mr. Billy!" she shouted, "It's Sandy, sweetie!" and she made her way on in.

He was old. But he looked even older than he was. He looked like it hurt him just to turn his head. Not because he was sick or something, but because he was sitting in the same position for so long he got stuck in it. He was like a statue carved into his worn-out chair. But he wasn't watching over nothing.

Sandy breezed in and gave him a kiss on the top of his head.

"Hello there, handsome!" she said affectionately. "This is my new intern, Jesse."

He picked up his glasses. I swear I heard his bones creak.

"Hi!" I shouted.

Sandy startled and gave me a look like, *not* that *loud*, then headed toward the kitchen area.

There was dust gathering on Mr. Billy's shoulders. His glasses were missing the parts that go on your ears to hold them up. I saw remnants of where he had tried to duct tape them together, but it hadn't worked, so he just held them up in front of one eye, the right one, because the blue part of his left eye was all covered in white. He squinted at me, and I briefly wondered why he didn't get new glasses when it was so obvious that all he did was read books. He was completely surrounded by them. In fact, I figured there were more books packed into that mobile home than there were at the Fort Scott Public Library.

The air was thick with pipe smoke, and I tried hard to not think about how sick it made me feel. I let my eyes wander around his home. I could see from one end to the other from right there in the middle. The kitchen was on one end, and on the other was a big bay window with shelves on either side of it. You could hardly see out the window due to all the stuff piled up on the seat in front of it.

There were books, but then there were all kinds of desert plants sitting on top of them and hanging from the ceiling too. The kind that don't need much water. Cactus and yucca and some spiny-looking ones. The plants were gathering dust too. He also had dried herbs and flowers and some braided prairie grass hanging on the walls and from the ceiling. I had to smile.

"You like that dried grass?" he interrupted my looking. I

jumped. It was more like a command than a question due to his loud, forced way of talking. It sounded like he had to work so hard at it to breathe that the words came out like he was shooting them. "Well, you must," *breath* "'cause I see you" *breath* "smiling at it."

He can see me? I stood there like a spooked jackrabbit, not knowing what to say. Ears alert.

He had some other weird stuff hanging there too—like dried-out snake skins and deer ribs. One wall of shelves was filled with wooden flutes and turtle-shell rattles. I was thinking how much I'd love to have a turtle shell in my barn when he shot words at me again.

"I make my own instruments," he said. "Out of stuff," *breath* "I find in the woods. You like music?" This time I was pretty sure he had asked a question.

"I—I think so," I said.

"You *think* so! Where d'ya get these kids, Sandy?"

Sandy just laughed. She'd started in cleaning up the pile of dirty dishes in the sink.

"Leave that shit, darling," *breath* "leave it. You're too good for housework."

"Whatever you say, handsome," Sandy said, but she kept on cleaning.

I recognized a book I saw laying midway through a dusty pile by the turtle shells.

"Hey," I said, "I know this one—we were supposed to read it at school, but my folks didn't let me."

He made a motioning signal with his arm for me to hand it to him, then felt it in his hands.

"Ah, Christ!" he cried out, "What were they afraid you'd learn, something about," *breath* "grass and nature and all that bullshit? They don't teach the best parts," *breath* "at school anyway."

"Language, Mr. Billy," Sandy sing-songed from the far end of the room.

"Oh, shit," he mumbled under his breath. "Here—*this* is the one you should read." He opened the book to a dog-eared page and held it out to me. Then he took it back before I could grab it. "Ah, hell, *I'll* read it to you."

He coughed so loud I worried something would come out of him. Like a lung. Then he started reading.

"Out of the cradle endlessly rocking, out of the mocking-bird's throat, the musical shuttle,

out of the Ninth-month midnight..."

At first I just couldn't believe he could see the words on the page because he wasn't holding his glasses, but then I realized he was reading by heart. His voice was still rough, but instead of shooting the words out, he fell into a rhythm with them. I listened like I was accustomed to listening to Dad's sermons. But these words were so different, the rhythm so new. I found myself concentrating on what they meant.

"Now in a moment I know what I am for, I awake..."

I focused so hard on figuring out what it meant that I forgot how uncomfortable I felt.

"Never more the cries of unsatisfied love be absent from me..."

The rhythm started to make a new pathway in my body. It was strange, like Sandy's music. I couldn't take my eyes off him. His grotesque left eye, his wrinkled neck, his hands, thick and covered with brown spots, barely holding onto the book. I started to get dizzy, the smell of pipe smoke churned with nerves in my stomach. I wanted to sit down, but I couldn't find a place that wasn't covered in stuff. The sound of Sandy running water and clanking dishes sounded far off in the distance. I thought I heard her laugh or maybe hum.

"That strong and delicious word which, creeping to my feet, or like some old crone rocking the cradle, swathed in sweet garments, bending aside, the sea whisper'd me."

He finished the poem, clapped the book shut, laid it on his

lap, and looked at me, boring into my head with the one blue eye. The smell of dish detergent and dried grass filled my nostrils, and my senses cleared.

"That sounded like music," I said.

"Hmph," he responded, "so you're not sure if you like it. Here." He shoved the book at me.

I took it up right away for fear of his arm giving out with him holding it up like that.

"Take it. Read it outside." He was back to shooting words. "Read it out loud. Ah hell, don't pay attention to an old man. You're young. It's a gift. Your momma teach you how to receive a gift?"

Of course she had, so I thanked him politely, even though I'd never heard so many swear words at one time in my life and I didn't know if I should be talking to him. Sandy, on the other hand, looked pleased as punch as she came gliding over to us from the sink. She had used her magic with the kitchen because in the course of one poem the dishes were washed and put away and the stench that had hung in the house when we arrived was gone.

"You have enough to eat, sweetie?" Sandy leaned down and asked Mr. Billy.

He waved his hand up and tried to brush her comment away.

"Stop your worrying, darling. I'm fine. I'm fine." He was pretending to be annoyed–it was clear he liked the attention. "You know," he creaked toward me like he didn't want Sandy to hear what he was about to say, "she doesn't really need to check up on me. She only comes because she likes me." His eye sparkled.

"Why don't you move into town?" Sandy asked with a wink. "Then I can visit you more often."

"Not a chance, darling."

"Never hurts to ask. See you next week then, sweetheart."

I sort of half smiled and lifted the book up, showing that I still had it, and we stepped out into the fresh air of the fully living again, leaving Mr. Billy to sit and decompose in his seat.

"So, what'd ya think?" Sandy asked as we climbed inside the baking car.

"I...don't know," I concluded.

Sandy laughed, "Well, it gets weirder!"

"You didn't do any nursing—I mean—did we drive all the way out here to do his dishes?"

"No—didn't you know? You did the nursing that time," Sandy said.

"What?"

"People need to talk to other people. To remember what it feels like to have something to say, to be listened to. People need other people who have something in common with them. That's good medicine."

"Does he have children to look after him?" I asked.

"He has children," Sandy said, "but they don't look after him." She looked down at her hands on the wheel and was silent for a moment. "Life is complex, kid."

I picked up the Brown Bomber at Sandy's office and began the drive home. The memory of Mr. Billy's white eye blurred with the passing storm ditch full of cheat grass, a dead raccoon, circling turkey vultures. The sound of wheels on road morphed into rock music in my brain. I wasn't sure how I would convince Dad to let me keep working with Sandy all summer when all I had to show for it was a mix CD and a book of poetry. But I was itching to read it to Sam. Maybe he was writing poetry in that book of his. Maybe we could sit under the cottonwoods by the tracks and read together, waiting for the next train to come by, hinting about whether or not we should hop on.

A shadow fell over the blinding light of late afternoon and felt like a cool cloth on my brain. Then lightning flashed. Just little flares of light at first, but as the sky grew darker, the streaks that connect the Earth to Heaven started in. I leaned forward in my seat and smiled up at the flashing sky. The lightning came strong and fast and so bright. I squinted my eyes.

I slowed down to watch the skies and smell the electric air. I wasn't paying attention and almost didn't see him. I broke hard—it was Sam, walking down the side of the highway, away from our house. I pulled over and peered out the passenger's side window at him. Something about him looked different as he gazed under his furrowed brow. I waved him in the car. He opened the door and a soury-sweet smell wafted in that I could only guess was alcohol. He stood at the open door for a long minute, slowly shifting his gaze from me to the road. Then thunder clapped so loud it shook the car and he got in real quick. He smelled even worse confined in the Buick and I knew I shouldn't take him home smelling like that.

"Where do you want to go?" I asked plainly.

"I don't know," he said, shaking his head.

I put the car in gear and drove out past the house, up the farm road to the ranch property. We pulled up on top of a ridge where you could see the entire sky. I turned off the engine and looked out at the storm. Mom and I used to go out stargazing there all the time when I was younger. I used to think it was the sky of the entire world. Sam slurped something out of a paper bag.

"Where'd you get that?" I asked.

"Missouri," he grunted.

"You walked all the way to Missouri?"

"Hitchhiked."

The storm played out in front of us, with lightning striking the ground all over the plain and thunder clapping up above. We sat in silence, and I counted the seconds between lightning and thunder crashes, wondering how soon the eye of the storm would reach us. *It's finally going to rain*, I thought. The car shook as the storm moved closer.

"Pull your feet up off the ground," Sam declared, searching the sky. He looked scared.

"I don't think that actually works," I said. "The tires are rubber and–"

He interrupted me by breathing out loud and heavy. I took in a breath to say something, but I didn't know what. So I looked out at the storm and tried to make my insides feel less electric than the lightning. It didn't work. I closed my eyes, wishing I had Sandy's CD to break the silence. The thought of that voice–the raw, human voice, the driving drums, the urgency of it all pulsed through my body.

The upholstery creaked as I shifted in my seat. I felt green eyes on my skin and I turned to look at him. Sam's eyes were red and tear-filled. I pulled the rubber band out of my ponytail and let my hair tumble down around my shoulders.

"Um," I managed to mumble. "Do you want to talk about it?" He shook his head.

I decided he needed some water. There was a bottle in the back seat, and I leaned toward him to grab it. His body froze as I almost brushed against him. He watched me twist in the seat to grab it and relaxed when I handed it to him. He chugged the water the same way he chugged the sun tea the first night I met him, and again I watched his Adam's apple move up and down when he tossed his head back to get the last drops.

"What do write about in your notebook?" I ventured.

He shrugged. "Thoughts. Poems. I shouldn't have gotten in the car," he said. "I'll get out here." He opened the door. The air froze for a moment. Then a crack of thunder shattered the sky. We both jumped, and I reached up and covered my ears and pulled my feet up onto the seat. I leaned across Sam, my knees pushing in on the emergency break and the seat belt poking into my ribs, and slammed the door shut.

"Don't get out now!" I shouted.

Sam took a deep breath then turned in the seat and looked straight at me. Lightning blazed in a whirlpool around us. Little hairs on the back of my neck stood on end and my insides buzzed in rhythm with the flickering light. I knew Mom and Dad would think it was wrong for me to be thinking thoughts about Sam the way I was thinking them. The way I had been thinking them since he hopped off the freight car. I shouldn't be looking at his green eyes for so long or staring at the tattoo peeking out of the top of his T-shirt or wondering what it feels like to kiss someone. I knew they would say it was wrong, like they had so many times before, like they kept saying about Missy. But for the life of me, in that moment, I couldn't figure out why.

Maybe Sam noticed the way I was looking at him because his gaze changed. His heart beat so hard I could see his shirt vibrate with its rhythm. I unbuckled my seatbelt. He had a concentrated look on his forehead, like he was trying to figure something out. He reached over and touched my bare leg, ever so gently, with his fingertips.

"Jesse," he half mumbled.

I thought a bolt of lightning had hit the car and raced through me. I touched his hand, hardly aware I was in control of my body, and leaned toward him.

He leaned in too and put his top lip right in between mine. It was soft at first. Softer and warmer than I imagined. He lifted his strong hand and covered the back of my head and neck, pulling me closer to him. Then he started making his way into my mouth with his tongue. It tasted awful—just like it smelled. I thought I might faint, trapped somewhere between disgust and ecstasy. He squeezed my leg with his other hand. I inched toward him and reached around to touch the back of his neck. I had wanted to touch the back of his neck since he first sat at our table.

We kept kissing, and he cupped my head with both hands. I felt buoyant. I couldn't help myself—I mean, I didn't plan it, but I ran my hands down his shirt and felt the muscles in his back. Then I just kept going and moved my hands around his sides.

Then, he pulled away. "I'm sorry, Jesse," he was breathing heavy. "God, I'm so sorry."

He might have been sorry, but I wasn't. In fact, I felt just like the lightning burning up the night. The current travelled down from the skies, through the hard ground, up through the honest-to-goodness rubber tires of the Brown Bomber, straight through the soles of my feet, and into my bloodstream. And it stayed. I still feel it now.

"What are you sorry for?" I asked. I wanted to set him straight. Let him know he didn't need to feel sorry for kissing a preacher's daughter.

"I shouldn't have done that," he said.

"It's okay, Sam. I wanted to," I assured him.

"I know—Jesse—you're so young," he stumbled. "*I* didn't want to." He turned away and grated his hands across his face. It looked like he sobered up real quick.

"Then why did you?" I asked.

"I don't know. It just sort of happened. Don't you see, Jesse?" He rubbed his face again. "Do you have any idea how many girls want to kiss me? I'm just—used to doing it. I wasn't thinking, that's all."

I stared at him. The realization that I was one on some long list of girls wanting to kiss Sam settled into my stomach, and I felt nauseous and stupid and ordinary.

"Why did you get off the train and come up to our house?" I almost whispered, staring ahead at the steering wheel.

"You want the truth?"

I nodded.

"I heard your mom's voice." He gulped. "The train stopped, and when it got quiet, I could hear your mom talking about being a woman. Her voice—it's soothing. It sounded like the voice of a woman that I would—that I would want to be with. Forever. It sounded like the voice of the natural woman. I don't know how to explain it, Jesse. I'd been reading a bunch of Kerouac and doing all this crazy stuff. I thought that—I guess I thought that maybe *she* was the whole reason why I had jumped on that freight car back in Portland to begin with. That fate, or something like that, had brought me here to meet her. I didn't think about anything after that. I just got off the train and went toward her."

He had been staring up at the lightning, replaying the moment in his head, but at that point he paused to look at me.

"It wasn't until after I started walking toward the house that I realized she was a mom. And a wife. That it was all just a fantasy in my head. But I thought—you know, I thought I could save her from this place. And it's not just a fantasy and—I don't know, Jesse. You're here, dressed in her clothes, and it all went wrong anyway already." He looked at me like he thought I understood. Like he had cleared the air and now everything was fine.

I took him in for a minute—his drunk eyes, his arrogant nod, his beautiful jaw, his sunburned hands. Then I spoke.

"Get out of my car."

5

LIES

It didn't rain.

I left Sam standing there on the plateau, lightning coming down all around him.

When I walked in the house Mom was standing at the oven, as usual. The smell of cornbread filled my nose. She was humming to herself. She had her grandma's apron on, the one she used when she wanted to look real nice and knew she wouldn't spill anything. I stood there for a moment before she noticed me, wondering what she would look like if she weren't my mom. Wondering what Sam was talking about when he said he wanted to be with her.

I tried to imagine I was looking at her for the first time. Her hair was pulled up, and her neck was soft and white, with little wisps of hair dangling down it. She would have looked curvy if she weren't so slender. She was affected—I could see it for the first time—by what, exactly, I didn't know. She looked like a housewife. There was a sadness flowing just underneath the humming. She had a presence, though; the whole room was full of a feeling that entered your body and stayed there as long as she did, a feeling that made you think you were special—the most special person in the world. A feeling that made you forget all the bad things you had thought or done.

I knew then it was that feeling Sam was in love with. He could feel it all the way over inside the freight car; of course he could. For the first time I resented her for that feeling.

Just then Mom turned around and saw me.

"Well, look who's back!" she said with a big smile. "I made your favorite!"

I burst into tears.

"Oh, honey!" She ran to me and hugged me real tight. "You must've had a really hard day."

"No," I sobbed into her shoulder, "I had a good day. It's something else."

"What is it, honey?" She stepped back and looked me over. "Are you okay? Are you hurt?" She was real worried. I had to tell her, otherwise she would be even more worried and never stop asking me about it.

"Is Dad home?" I asked.

"No, he's sorry, honey, but he has to miss dinner. He's counseling the Thomas boy—" she sighed, "for some reason."

"You have to promise not to tell him any of this. I mean not one part of it, Mom." I was serious, and it worried her enough to actually promise, which I knew she didn't want to—she never kept anything from Dad.

"I promise," she half whispered, ushering me to the couch. We sat down, and I took a deep breath.

"Well," I began, "I had this crush on someone. I mean, I really *really* liked this person. I thought—I thought maybe I was even in love with them," I alluded. Mom started looking relieved. "But it turned out that this person was in love with someone else."

"This person," Mom said tentatively, "are they—getting married—soon?"

"It ain't Missy, Mom!" I blurted.

She was so relieved she didn't even correct my grammar.

She stroked my hair. "Is it a boy from school?"

"It's no one from school, Mom. I just feel so stupid," I whispered. Just then I heard the door creak behind me and a look came across Mom's face that I'd never seen before. What was it? Shame? I turned around, and there was Sam, swaying in the doorway.

He held his arm up on the doorframe to steady himself, and my face burned. My mind spun thinking of what to do.

"So, she's told you everything, now, hasn't she?" he slurred at us.

Oh, please don't, I thought.

"I didn't mean to *kiss* her. It just sort of happened, I swear."

Too late. He said it. Mom looked downright horrified. I braced myself for her anger, disgust, or, worse yet, her disappointment in me, but she stood up, breezed right past me, and marched up to Sam.

"You—kissed my *daughter*?" she hissed through clenched teeth. "You should be ashamed of yourself! She's *eight* years younger than you! How could you even *think* of doing such a thing after—" She stopped herself and looked back at me.

"What d'you mean how could *I* think of *her*?" Sam protested. "*She* thought of *me*."

Oh God! That was the last thing I wanted him to say.

"And furthermore," he continued, "you're *eight* years older than *me*!"

I didn't see what that had to do with anything. Mom turned around and looked at me, her eyes a well of pain. I thought I would die if she looked like that because of me.

"I'm eight years older than you," she whispered. Her eyes hardened, and she turned to Sam again. "You're drunk," she said. "Go pack your things, and I'll give you a ride to Fort Scott. You can't stay in this house anymore."

"Oh, I see," Sam tripped past her, "like mother, like

daughter. Use me and then push me away."

"This is just some stop on your little adventure—*we're* just some stop," Mom fumed. "Maybe you'll get a poem out of us for your book. But this is our *life*." She was seething. I thought she might spit fire.

"Don't bother giving me a ride," Sam muttered over his shoulder on his way down the hall. "There's a train coming."

It was silent. I sat on the couch and waited for whatever was coming next, unable to even think past the shame of Mom knowing I had kissed Sam. She stood staring after him with her back toward me.

Sam appeared in the hallway; backpack hitched over one shoulder. "Come with me," he said. Blood rushed into my ears and I sucked air in violent heaves. The decision hurled itself into my chest like a wrecking ball, I couldn't form words from it. I searched Sam's eyes for an indication of what to do.

He wasn't looking at me. He was looking at Mom.

"You're oppressed and you don't even know it!" he pleaded.

I heard the train pull up in front and come to a stop. Sam was right.

"Go." It sounded like a swear word coming from Mom's lips.

Sam strode across the living room without looking back. He hopped on that train just like I always thought he would and vanished. Just like that.

The front door stood open and cicada song drifted in. My heart ached. I could still feel his kiss in my body.

Mom paced to the door and closed it. "Let's talk, Jesse," she said, turning around. Her manner had become serious and quiet like Dad, and my heart jumped into my throat. Then she softened into herself. "First, let's eat," she said and got the cornbread out of the oven and set it on the table.

"Jesse," Mom said, buttering a piece for me, "there's

something I've always known I'd need to tell you one day, and I guess today is that day."

I gulped and took the bread she handed me.

"You heard Sam say I'm eight years older than him?" she asked.

"Uh-huh. I guess—I thought he was younger."

"No, hun, you heard me say—he's eight years older than you, and I'm eight years older than him," she said.

"That can't be," I said. "That'd mean you were only sixteen when I was born."

She stared at me.

"Hold on. What, exactly, are you telling me right now? Does this have anything to do with Sam and me?"

"No. Yes. Well, in a way it does. It's related, honey. It's important that you learn from my mistakes," she stammered.

Mom never stammered. My breath cut off. I felt dizzy. I rested my elbows up on the table and leaned over my plate.

"Just say it, Mom," I mumbled. "Just say whatever it is you're trying to say."

"When you were born, Jesse," she resumed Dad's calmness, "I was only sixteen years old. Your father and I weren't married yet. We didn't get married until after you were born. We were in high school."

I stared at my cornbread. It was still steaming. They lied to me. It's all I could think of. They lied. And that's a sin.

"Say something, please, honey," Mom pleaded.

"You lied."

"Well, we didn't exactly lie, honey. We never meant to—"

"You lied to me. You told me you got married, moved out here, and then I was born. You can't say that's not true—that's how it's always been told."

"Honey, we always knew we would tell you when you were old enough, but that's not something you can just tell a child. You needed to be a young woman." She sighed. She looked disappointed. This isn't how she wanted the conversation to happen. She wanted to be in charge of how I found out—not some rail hopper who came in and forced the issue.

"So tell me now," I said. "What's the truth?"

Mom looked up at the ceiling—I think she was praying—then back down at the table.

"We had you first. Then we got married, and Dad joined the seminary. After he graduated we moved out here so—so we could start fresh and no one would judge us. We just—we started over. And you didn't have a choice, but you started over too. We put you in kindergarten—see, we just didn't want anyone asking us questions about it—your father, with his job—we were so young—people depend on him to be a voice—to have high moral principles—"

"What are you talking about?"

"You're sixteen, Jesse."

"*What?*" I pushed my plate across the table at her. "I'm what?" I stood up.

"You're sixteen." All the color had left Mom's face. She looked like she was going to be sick.

"How could you and Dad go on about Missy?" I whispered. "You did the exact same thing. How could you tell me I was sinning to think about—to want to—"

"It's exactly *because* we know what it's like that we wanted to protect you from what we did and what Missy did," her voice rose in pitch.

"You have no right! I'm not like you!" I shouted. But I wondered if it was true, even as I said it. I wondered what would have happened if Sam would have liked me back; if we would have kept kissing in the lightning storm. Sam. His suntanned neck entered my thoughts and I pushed it away. Sam. He told Mom she was eight years older than him. A new and horrific thought entered my mind.

"Oh my God," I swore, and I didn't even care. "What did

you do with Sam?"

"Oh honey–"

"Oh no–just tell me. He told me he was in love with you. What happened between you two?"

"He told you what?" she whimpered. She looked panicked. She pushed her plate back and threw her napkin on top of it. When she spoke it came out flustered, scattered. "I am not just your mother. I am a person. I have a right to a private life. I don't appreciate you questioning me like this!"

"I don't appreciate you keeping an entire year of my life secret!" I shouted.

She stood up and put her hands on her hips. I reared back.

"I am the same person I was ten minutes ago, Jesse!" She pointed to the living room. "I love you. I love your father, but life is not so simple!" She gestured down the hall. "*This* is a process. Humans have feelings." She threw her hands against her chest. "Sometimes–unexpected feelings."

"Do you even love Dad? Did you *want* to marry him? Or did you *have* to because of me?"

The color returned to Mom's face. She took a deep breath. "Both those things are true," she said. With that she turned from the table and retreated to her domain: the kitchen sink. She turned on the hot water and began filling the sink with soap suds.

I wanted to scream. I wanted to break something. I wanted to run outside and hop on the train. Instead, I sat down, wondering what to say and do and think.

"Here it is, Jesse," Mom said, leaving the water running, steam pouring up in her face. "You don't want lies? Here's the truth." She turned and looked me straight in the eye.

Oh God, do I want the truth? I wondered.

"I was a regular girl, Jesse, just like you. I had crushes on boys, most of all Rocky Hendricks, and I didn't think that made me any less God-fearing or God-loving. I was a pious girl." She turned the water off and started scouring a pan. "This sounds so stupid now, but your grandpa, my dad, well, he found out I was at the prom with Rocky. He was always so busy with the farm, he never paid attention before." She worked fast, and it made her voice shake with her body as she scraped steel wool across the pan. "But somehow he caught wind that I was out with Rocky, and we hadn't shown up to the dance—you remember how his truck broke down. Rocky never knew his daddy—he had left when he was a baby—but it turned out his daddy was a migrant worker on our farm. Grandpa knew him. And when I came home that night after we got the truck working, Grandpa pulled me into the barn and slapped me so hard I was seeing stars."

She scrubbed the pot with such fierceness I thought she would scratch a hole in it. Metal tore metal, and Mom's voice rose above it. "He forbade me from seeing him again. I was never so scared in my life. He'd never acted like that toward me before and never did since, even after—well, even after everything. I was so mad at him, Jesse, for treating me like that. For judging Rocky without even knowing him. But I didn't dare disobey him. When your father showed up a couple months later, I took one look at him and knew he was the perfect way to get back at Grandpa. Blond hair and a lost look in his blue eyes. His parents had sent him to live with his grandma in Independence to try to straighten him out, get him away from the gangs in Wichita."

"Dad? *Gangs?*"

"He wasn't always a preacher, you know. Dad was a million times more dangerous than poor Rocky—but he was white, so Grandpa couldn't say anything about it. I wanted out of Independence, the same way you want out of here—don't think I don't know—so I walked up to your dad the first day he was in class and asked him to meet me behind the bleachers after school. A stupid grin crossed his face, and I knew that was that. He didn't even need to speak." She let the pan go and rubbed streaks of black grease on her grandma's apron.

"You question whether I loved your dad or not? After a few months I loved him so much I lost myself in him. All I wanted was to be around him. But Dad wasn't the first person I was in love with—Rocky was. Do you know what we did out there in the Milo fields on prom night?" Tears filled her eyes and she choked out the next words. "We danced. We danced, and it was beautiful. And I always felt bad about the way we broke up." She wiped the tears from her cheeks with the back of her hand.

"Jesse, my point is, is that people don't start out to do things that are going to hurt others. They don't start out thinking about sinning. But bad feelings or hurt feelings can send us in all kinds of crazy directions. I'm glad I married your father. I'm glad I had you—more glad than anything in the world." She took a deep breath and cleared her throat.

"Being married doesn't mean you completely lose feelings for other people. You have to contend with them, you *want* to contend with them. Sometimes it's harder than others. Sam—" she sighed.

My stomach lurched into my throat.

"Sam reminded me of Rocky, I guess. At least the way he looked at me reminded me of him. Sam reminded me of the girl I used to be, before I lost myself. I love taking care of you and Dad, that's my choice, but it's not the only thing about me. I'm a woman, a regular woman. I liked the way Sam made me feel because I could tell he liked *me*." She looked out the window into the dark backyard.

"I didn't think—I swear, Jesse, I didn't know you liked him—I thought of him as being too old for you to consider. I didn't think anything would come of it—I didn't think..." She picked up a washcloth and mindlessly dipped it in and out of the steaming water.

"One day, out by the shed, Sam told me why he got off the train. You know what he did?" she laughed with no humor. "He asked me to dance. I don't honestly know what he thought would happen. I don't know what I thought would happen. He kissed me, and..." She wrung the cloth. Then she filled a glass with cold tap water. It felt like it took a million years for the water to reach the top. Her hands were raw and red, they shook as she held the glass to her lips. She gulped the water down all at once like Sam did in the Buick, then she set the glass on the counter and just looked at it.

"What happed after that is between Sam and me," she whispered, not taking her eyes off the glass.

The kitchen spun. I wanted to throw up. I stumbled up from my chair, *my* chair at *my* kitchen table, but it wasn't mine anymore. Everything looked the same, but it was a different chair in a different house.

"Oh my God," I managed to squeak, holding my stomach. "Mother—it was you—that night it got so hot. That night Sam was sitting outside my window, he wasn't alone—it was you. You were out there with him."

"Jesse," Mom whispered and bent her head down, gripping the kitchen counter with her hands and leaning on it.

Her words swarmed through my head like insects. The lies. The fact that she wanted Sam the same way I did. The fact that she had done things with him. I couldn't even pick which part shocked me the most. I didn't know if it was Sam, or Dad, or even Grandpa hitting Mom like that. My heart beat against the inside of my head, I couldn't breathe. A searing pain began creeping its way down from my temple to the nape of my neck. I stumbled into the living room and grabbed the car keys from the coffee table.

"I'm not regular," is all I said, and I turned around and walked out the front door.

6

A NEW LOVE OF YOUR LIFE

I drove.

I didn't know where I was going. Away—away from her. I wanted to cry, but tears wouldn't come. My mind spun around and around and kept landing on one question: was my whole life—my very existence—was it all based on a sin? On Mom trying to get back at Grandpa?

The wind whipped my hair against my cheeks and shouted at me. The lightning had gone, and it still never rained; the sky was now a moonless black. Mom's words spun out of the tires like bees and grinded against the pavement. Her pale face, Sam's breath—they crowded against me.

I ended up at Sandy's townhouse. It was one of a long row of townhomes, all painted the same blue gray with white trim that was chipping off. She had pointed it out to me that morning when we passed by. I had never been there before, but I could guess which door was Sandy's: There was a foot-tall statue of the Keeper of the Plains sitting in the windowsill and two bowls of cat food set out on the stoop.

I don't know how long I stood there, studying the shapes of the cat food, trying to decide if I should knock. Finally,

Sandy opened a window.

"You gonna come in?" she called. I opened my mouth to answer, but my chest stole my breath and pushed it down to my stomach. Instead, I doubled over, gripped my belly, and tried to hold my body together as heaving sobs tore through my throat.

Sandy didn't ask what happened. She led me into a small, rectangular apartment, kitchen on one side and TV on the other. Her hand, firm around my shoulders, helped contain the heaving, which moved into my head and turned to whirling upon entering the warmth of the room. There was soft, warm light burning all around and stacks of old records, CDs, books, and papers on every flat surface. Stereo speakers, end tables, countertops, chairs—they were all covered. The walls were busy with art—photographs of dancers; drawings; paintings of old, twisted wood; a tambourine; and some sculptures that looked like different-shaped lumps to me. A high shelf along the entire back wall was lined with woven baskets. There was so much to take in that my body became distracted, and the whirling sobs turned to normal crying as I gazed around the room.

It smelled like cooking dinner and burnt incense. The TV was turned on to the news; they were talking about the drought. An orange cat jumped up on top of the TV and began licking itself.

Sandy led me to the table, a small round one separating the kitchen from the living area. There was already a woman seated there.

"I'm sorry," I said through wet eyes. "I didn't know you had company."

Sandy smiled. "That's not company," she said, patting the woman on her back, "This is Bonita. She lives here."

I tried to say it was a pleasure to meet her, but I couldn't get the words out on account of the crying. It took over once again and shook my body in waves. Sandy shooed a black cat off the seat next to Bonita, sat me down, and went to the kitchen to make tea. I gasped between sobs and tried to find my breath.

Bonita was slightly older than Sandy and wore the same colorful, flowy clothes. Her hair sprayed out from behind her round face in thick, black and gray curls. She was looking over some papers.

"You're upset, honey," Bonita said to me, patting my hand. "We can do our introductions later. But I must say you don't really need introducing—I feel like I know you already." Her low, deliberate voice had a calming effect on me.

There was a little counter between the kitchen and the table, and Sandy squeezed around it, holding a tray of teacups and a hot kettle. Bonita bent her head down to look up at Sandy over the top of her reading glasses.

"Maybe I should take my tea to our room so you and Jesse can talk," she said.

"Thank you, love," Sandy said with a soft smile.

It was then I realized Bonita was in a wheelchair. Sandy pulled her back from the table and wheeled her down the hall and into a doorway behind the kitchen. I guessed that was the bedroom. I wondered why Sandy never mentioned Bonita before. Everything about her house was so different than ours. It was untidy, mismatched, jam-packed full of weird stuff, and wonderful. Suddenly I didn't know Sandy at all. There was a trumpet hanging on the wall in the hallway.

"Do you play the trumpet?" I asked when Sandy came back down the hall.

"No! Bonita found that old thing at a garage sale and thought it would look cool on the wall. Here, drink." She handed me the tea. "There's a holey violin and some maracas in the bathroom, if you're interested." She scuttled around a bit, turning the TV off, picking up papers, shooing cats, sneezing, and lighting candles, until she settled in with her cup of tea across from me.

"So," she asked, "what's going on?"

Where did I start? With Mom? With the kiss? Could I really tell my parents' secret? Could I tell my own? I resolved to keep quiet. But then I took one sip of tea and blurted it out anyway.

"He was walking down the road and I picked him up and we were watching the lightning—Sam, I mean. I really liked him—and I kissed him, and he was drunk, but then he said he was in love with my *mom* and then she said—and then I found out that Mom and Dad have been lying to me—this whole time." My voice rose higher and higher as I said it all, and by the end I could barely get the squeaking words out before I began sobbing again.

"Okay," Sandy said slowly, not looking surprised at all. "That's a lot, sweetie. Keep drinking the tea. Where's Sam now?"

"Mom kicked him out. He hopped on a train."

"Does your mom know you're here?"

"No."

"Do I have your permission to call her and let her know you're safe?"

"I guess," I said.

Sandy went back to her room, and I could vaguely hear her phone voice.

"Come on, now," she said into the phone, "don't beat yourself up. That doesn't help anyone."

She came back with a big sigh and clapped her hands. "Well, then, let's eat dinner!"

"I don't think I'm hungry," I said.

"Okay, you sit. Bonita and I will eat," she said.

Bonita made her way down the narrow hall with surprising ease and took her place at the table. "You can talk about it if you want," she said over her glasses, "but you don't have to." I nodded. "Sometimes saying things out loud makes them smaller."

It was weird watching Sandy cook. At our house Mom cooked for her, but in her own kitchen, it was clear Sandy was in charge. It occurred to me she was in charge everywhere she went.

"This is Bonita's favorite," Sandy said with a smile when she sat down.

The food she cooked was from another planet than my mother's. She used spices and other weird things I'd never heard of like lentils and poblano peppers. I closed my eyes and held my hands out to pray. The sound of fork against plate filled my ears, and my hands remained empty. I opened my eyes, and Sandy smiled kindly and patted my hand.

"I'm sixteen," I said blankly, tears streaming gracefully.

Sandy raised her eyebrows and set her fork down. "They lied to you about how old you are?" she asked.

I nodded. "Among other things." Sandy and Bonita looked at each other.

"Eat," Sandy said and resumed eating herself.

I forced myself to take a few bites, out of courtesy, then had to gulp a sea of water to get my mouth to cool down. Sandy and Bonita exchanged glances in silence. I poked at my pepper with my fork. I decided I didn't want to talk about it, even if it would make it smaller.

"What are all these papers for?" I asked, changing the subject.

"I'm a proofreader," Bonita said.

"Oh, *that's* why this place is covered with paper," Sandy teased.

Bonita rolled her eyes.

"Oh. Do you like it?" I asked.

"Well," she set down her fork, "it's a job." Then she got a little sparkle in her eyes. "I used to be a dancer." She glanced up at a photograph on the wall behind my head. I turned around to look at it.

It was her—a much younger version, but it was her. She had a long, flowy skirt on with a black leotard. One leg was raised high up above her head, and she was balanced on the ball of her other foot. She was barefoot. Her head was thrown back, and long, black curls spun out around her. She had a giant flower pinned in her hair above her ear. There was pain in her expression, even though her body looked so strong. Her hands looked like they were grasping for something, but all they could grab onto was air. She was beautiful.

"Dancing was the love of my life," she said.

I wanted to ask what happened, how she ended up in a wheelchair, but I didn't know how.

"I developed MS, and I had to stop dancing," she read my mind.

I looked at the photo for a moment. The strength, the emotion, the power. I could see the love. "How do you manage?" I asked. "I mean, without that love?"

Bonita gave a faint smile and shook her head. "I had to find a new love of my life," she said and looked at Sandy.

Sandy got up and started clearing the table. She brought out a cup of tea and set it down real gently in front of Bonita.

"Life rarely goes the way you think it should," Sandy said.

"That's true," Bonita echoed, "but you'll get through it." She had tears in her eyes, but they weren't sadness alone; there was something else in there too. "Take our Sandy here," she said, changing her tone, "she started as a rock star."

"Oh, please," Sandy quipped, "I was always better at people than I was at rhythm. We all have talents, right, Jesse?"

She set another cup of tea in front of me. I drank, and my mind slowed down. Memories of kissing Sam were still flashing through my blood in jagged bolts, but something in the tea made me relax.

All the tension in my body flowed down my spine and out the soles of my feet, but suddenly it was too much leaving all at once. My head, which moments before had been pounding and spinning, became light and floaty. It felt like it was floating up to the ceiling. I wondered if it would detach from my neck and blood would pour out over Sandy's kitchen table. I drew a curtain around my brain, trying to keep my head on, and Sandy spoke from behind it.

"I think I told you, Jesse, when I was your age, I had to support my mom. She drank a lot—couldn't keep a job. My dad had gone back to the reservation years before that. I worked at the fish hatchery after school and on weekends. But still kept my grades up so I could leave some day. It wasn't easy."

Bonita reached out and ran her thumb along a scar on the back of Sandy's hand. It was a gentle movement.

"I almost didn't finish school at all. To be honest, I'm pretty lucky to be alive. My mom—she wasn't herself when she was drinking. She let people in our lives she shouldn't have. Made some bad choices." She moved to the kitchen and scraped the food off the dishes. "But I loved her. Because she was my mom. And we can't help but love our moms, can we Jesse?" She turned the faucet on and watched the sink fill with water. "It was a rough time, but I got through it, and it brought me to where I am today, and I wouldn't change *that* for anything."

"Sandy, can I stay here tonight?" I asked, letting the invisible curtain roll down my head and cover my body.

"I was counting on it, sweetie," she smiled.

My eyelids closed and burned my eyes but wouldn't open. Strong hands ushered me toward the couch—maybe Sandy's, maybe not. Softness cushioned my head. I let go of trying to hold it on and floated into the night.

7

COLD FEET

"*Where* have you been, Jesse?"

"Mis, I have so much to tell you—"

"You have to try on your dress—and your shoes. We have to dye them to match, you're in charge of the altar flowers, and can your mom bake the cake? Here's a list—I'll be off in ten minutes, then we can go to JP's house—I mean, *home*, 'cause I live there now too, you know. Oh my God, I'm getting *married*!" Missy flitted away from me, hair sprayed up like a fountain on top of her head and feet turned out at an angle as she puttered around Juan Pablo's parents' restaurant. She started working there as a waitress when her parents kicked her out. I sat at the counter drinking a pop while she finished her shift.

Sandy, and Bonita, said I could stay with them as long as I wanted to. As long as it was okay with Mom and Dad. I guess Mom felt so bad about lying—and Sam—she agreed to it. The first thing I did was go see Missy.

She breezed up next to me holding two five dollar bills out for me to see before shoving them into her apron.

"People been giving me such good tips. Dang, ever since

my belly popped out, I'm making so much money! I could get you a job here if you want, Jesse. After graduation you could come work here, and we'd see each other every day! You could help babysit—it'll be so much fun!" She squeezed my arm and took a sip of my pop, then hurried off to the next table.

"Bye! Have a good day!" she called to a couple walking out the door.

I looked around at the cracked, red booths with bits of stuffing coming out; the dusty pictures of Old Mexico hanging on the walls; bus tub full of red, plastic cups, half filled with ice. Most of it had already been there when Juan Pablo's parents bought the restaurant. They left everything the same as the last restaurant except the food. The smell of refried beans wafted out from the back along with accordion music. I caught a glimpse of Juan Pablo working in the kitchen. I waved; he smiled.

"C'mon, girl!" Missy sucked the last drops of pop through the straw then took it back to the kitchen.

Juan Pablo kissed her belly and her lips, and then Missy waved for me to follow her out the door.

We sat in Juan Pablo's bedroom, which had been completely taken over by Missy's things, right down to the ruffled bedspread. It was like sitting in her same room, but in a different reality. Missy liked ruffles, which I really came to understand when I saw my bridesmaid's dress.

"You're my maid of honor, and that means you're my servant. Just kidding!" She paused a bit too long before saying the kidding part. Missy pulled a white, ruffled dress out for me to try on. "We have to dye it, of course, because you can't wear white—only the bride can wear white—but this one was on sale, and it's going to match the flowers—fuchsia—that means dark pink. We'll do your hair up—kind of like mine, but not so fancy. You'll look so pretty, Jesse. But not as pretty as me. Just kidding!"

The dress fit well enough, although *pretty* was not the word I would have used to describe it. Hideous seemed more accurate. I kept waiting for a break in conversation to tell Missy everything that had happened the day before. Everything about Sam, about rock music and poetry, about Mom and Dad and how she didn't need to feel bad because they did the exact same thing. But the thing was, Missy didn't feel bad. Missy was in a great mood. She got to make me and Juan Pablo wear whatever she wanted, she got to buy special makeup, she got to have a hairdresser do her hair. She liked working at the restaurant. The more I talked to her, the further I got from being able to confide in her.

So, I spent the day painting my toenails fuchsia, painting Missy's toenails rose because she couldn't reach them anymore, picking flowers for the altar, and running back and forth to the store to pick up things for Missy. When I finally left, the dress in all its ruffled glory, soaked in what looked like a sink full of blood in the back of the restaurant.

I drove home that evening to get my clothes and any other things I wanted to have at Sandy's. I knew Mom and Dad would be at Bible study. I left a note for Mom about the cake on our kitchen table. When I walked into the house I felt like a different person. It was quiet and tidy and seemed emptier than before. I glanced in Mom and Dad's room, and hot tears filled my eyes. My bed was made with clean sheets, and I knew Mom had been hanging out in my room. Mr. Billy's book lay there on the tattered quilt. I picked it up and took a walk out to the barn. I decided to read it out loud, just like Mr. Billy said to.

Sweat soaked the back of my hair and cooled my neck. I tucked the book in the back of my cutoffs and climbed the tree. When I got settled, I began to read. First to the scorched grass and mosquitoes—quietly, embarrassed to be doing it, then, as the rhythm of the words swirled around me, I read louder. The sound drifted through the branches then took on its own life, coursing up beneath my feet and making me feel stronger. Suddenly I wanted to wake up the parched, sleeping prairie. I wanted to make it green again. And I thought I might be able to. I stood up on the thick branch, book in one hand, hugging the trunk with the other, and I shouted the plains awake. Phrases like prayers swept from my mouth, crashed along the rainless grass, then pulled back again, entering my body, and tallying all the live parts of me.

Missy wanted to be married on the first day of summer. The longest day of the year. She was real good at thinking up romantic things like that. But it had already been so hot for the month of June it felt like August. Out of the myriad of options, the drought turned out to be the most annoying wedding guest.

The night before Missy's wedding the church's air conditioner broke. I found out because Dad called Sandy, hoping she could help. The repair company was closed already, and the next day was Saturday, which would cost extra. He was desperate to fix it, probably because if he didn't, he'd not only lose his own flock but also fail to convert all the Catholics who were showing up the next day for the wedding. Of the long list of people who were friends of Sandy's, not one was an air-conditioner repairman. Dad worked half the night until he gave up and took to praying.

All I could think of was poor Missy's styled-up wedding hair drenched with sweat and how uncomfortable she would be at seven months pregnant under all those ruffles. I felt a tinge of shame when I thought about how if Sam were still here, he'd have fixed it in no time. But what did Sam know about air conditioners anyway?

I went to tell Missy about the AC and do whatever it is that maids of honor are supposed to do the night before the wedding and found her raging over her shoes. Her feet had swollen, and the shoes didn't fit anymore. Juan Pablo looked exhausted.

"Baby, it doesn't matter. I don't care if you have shoes. Just go barefoot," he pleaded.

"Barefoot? *Barefoot*! I am not some trashy, barefoot bride!"

I decided not to tell her about the air conditioning. I whispered it to Juan Pablo while Missy dug through his closet, looking for more shoes. He looked at me with terror in his eyes, then left to go tell his parents.

"Don't worry, Mis," I said. "I'm a size bigger than you, right? I'll find some of my shoes for you."

"No offence, Jesse, but you have no clue about fashion. You don't have *any* nice shoes."

A friend loves at all times, and a sister is born for adversity, I thought.

Our church was small and old, just like Mom and Dad liked it. It had white-washed walls with small, wavy glass windows along the sides. At the front of the sanctuary was a stage with the pulpit, a piano, risers for the choir, and a giant wooden cross. Behind the stage to the right was a little room where Dad wrote his sermons and prepared for the service. This was where Missy and I were getting ready. There was a private bathroom in there, too, because nobody wants to pee next to a preacher.

In the dark, cool basement we had Sunday potluck meals after the service and wedding and funeral receptions. The morning of the wedding Mom was down there making it as pretty as she possibly could with two roles of pink crepe paper and the plastic tablecloths with tulips on them that were usually reserved for Easter.

Normally the sanctuary was bright, with sunlight seeping in through the opaque windows, but since the drought we'd hung up old sheets of varying colors to keep the heat out. Light snuck in wherever it could, trickling through worn-out places in the sun-bleached fabric and gushing through the openings between the sheet and the wall. It felt almost romantic in there. I wondered why some sheets were worn in certain places and whose bodies had worn them.

One hour before the wedding Dad became frantic. He paced up and down the aisle, like he was trying to create his own wind, soaked through and through with sweat. Mom set out water jugs and plastic cups in every corner, praying no one would suffer heat stroke. I peeked through the door from the back room and tried not to make eye contact. I still hadn't spoken to either one of them.

Missy and I sat in rolling office chairs in our underpants and bras, unable to conceive of putting on all those ruffles until the amen minute. Dad's desk was covered in powders and blushes and safety pins and changes of underpants and bobby pins. Missy was under the impression that there would be, at long last, some certain amount of hairspray that would be resistant to the heat. I held up her hair while she sprayed. I thought I might pass out from the fumes. Sweat glistened across her beach-ball belly and pooled in the space between her growing breasts. I walked to the door and opened it, then shut it, unable to determine which was the cooler option, and vaguely wondered if we were playing house or not.

Then the vaqueros arrived.

Juan Pablo and all the men in his family, dressed in fancy western shirts, boots, and cowboy hats, burst through the double doors like a cool breeze. They seemed resistant to the heat. They were festive, laughing even, teasing Juan Pablo and carrying on. They brought fans—window fans and table fans and fans on stands. And they brought ice. Big blocks of it from the restaurant. They set to work cooling that sanctuary down like it was their own. Dad was stunned. His prayers had been answered—by Catholics, Mexican Catholics.

There'd be no converting them now.

Then the women showed up. They looked beautiful. Juan Pablo's mother and aunts had multicolored dresses and jewelry that Mom would never let me wear. Suddenly Mom looked plain. Some of the girls had flowers pinned in their thick, dark hair. They brought beautiful, homemade, colored paper flowers and taped them on the ends of the aisles. The flowers fluttered in the wind from the fans like tropical birds. It was a miracle. I'd never seen the church look so beautiful. I threw on my ruffles to check it out and report back to Missy.

Mom was delighted. She asked an old woman to teach her how to make the flowers, and they were both tickled to pieces about it, sitting in front of a fan, folding paper together.

"Missy!" I grinned, closing the door behind me. "You're gonna *love* it! It's beautiful! There's flowers everywhere—"

She was crying.

"What's wrong, Mis?" I asked. The crying turned to sobbing. Her body lurched and shook, trying to get the tears out. Sweat ran down her giant belly in rivers, mascara poured down her cheeks, and her kinky blond hair was like a melted ice cream scoop on top of her head.

"I can't do it," she whispered.

Then, like the words themselves had injured her further, she started bawling.

"I!" she wailed, "CAN'T!" I thought she might be hyperventilating. "DO! IT!"

It was too hot to hug her, and I couldn't quite get my hands through her hair to stroke it, so I took the previous week's service program and fanned her while I laid my hand on her shoulder. I had no advice.

"Let's just both take a few deep breaths," I said.

She calmed a bit.

"You know how your daddy says we should thank God for the prayers he don't answer too?" she said.

"Sure, I guess."

"Well, maybe he's right," she said.

"What do you mean?" I asked.

"I don't know," she wailed. "Maybe I should've just waited for God instead of always stirring things up. Maybe Juan Pablo and I should've used a condom."

"What's a condom?"

"Oh. My. God, Jesse. Honestly, what on *earth* would you do without me?"

I always have appreciated the way Missy talked to me like I was a normal teenager and not a preacher's daughter like all the other kids did. Her lesson about condoms calmed her nerves a bit, but she still burst into tears when she reached the part about her getting pregnant. I recognized that this was out of my hands.

"Should I go get your dad?" I asked. Missy wasn't on good terms with her mom.

"Yes. I want to talk to Daddy," she said.

I found Missy's dad locked in conversation with my dad. He was getting advice about parenting a teenage mother. Something Dad knew a lot about, I thought sorely.

"'*We walk by faith, not by sight,*'" he was saying as I walked up.

"Missy needs to talk to you," I said, not looking at Dad.

Her dad looked scared. I didn't have the heart to tell him just how scared he ought to be.

I led him back to Missy. When he walked in the room and saw her crying he stopped right in the doorway. I stood beside her, resolve in my shoulders.

"I can't do it, Daddy," she cried, even as she was pulling on the dress. "I just don't think I'm ready for this."

"Now, Missy. C'mon, baby," her dad spoke to her with the same tone he used when we were kids and he was convincing her to let him rip a band-aid off. "There's a church full of people out there all ready to see you walk down the aisle in your beautiful dress," he said. "Ain't this everything you always wanted?" He inched away from the doorway, like he was trying to disappear. "Don't you got just the right bouquet and pretty dress and everything you wanted?"

"Yes, but—"

"Now, Jesse's mom worked hard to make you a beautiful cake—I saw it downstairs, baby. It's just pretty as a picture," he said.

I wanted to tell him he was missing the point, but I didn't know how. Missy started to calm herself down, thinking about all the pretty things.

"There's a pile of presents down there, baby. And ain't JP everything you wanted? You love him, don't you?"

"Yes, I love him, but—"

"Now, just look at how beautiful your hair is!" he went on. "You'll be fine, baby. You just have cold feet. There ain't a bride in the world who don't get cold feet on her wedding day."

Missy stopped crying completely. "There ain't?"

"No, that's normal, okay, baby? You okay now? You look beautiful. You're gonna be fine. This is what you wanted," he said. "You okay?" He was practically down the hallway.

"Yeah, Daddy. Thank you. I'm okay now," Missy said. Her dress was rumpled up around her breasts, halfway on, and her face was streaked black.

Her dad left, looking like he'd just barely escaped a painful death, and Missy started to work fixing her makeup.

"Are you sure?" I asked slowly.

"Yeah," she answered, wiping the mascara from her cheeks. "It's just cold feet, like Daddy said. It's probably the hormones, too."

"We could still eat the cake," I mumbled.

I helped her as best I could with her makeup. Shiny powder, glitter gloss, silvery-black eye shadow—she looked like she was going to the prom.

"Missy," I asked, brushing rouge across her cheek, "what does it feel like? To be in love?"

She laughed half-heartedly. "Oh, Jesse," she opened her eyes and looked at me a long minute. "It's different than you think," she said seriously. Then she closed her eyes. We stayed there for a quiet moment, listening to the buzz of people out in the sanctuary. *Maybe I don't know Missy at all,* I thought. Her eyes shot open.

"Oh my God, Jesse! I forgot it! I remember I put it on the dresser when I was getting my dress out, and then I forgot to pick it back up! JP's ring! Oh my God!"

"Don't panic!" I said, fearing a repeat of crying and comforting and reapplying. "I'll go get it, Missy. Don't worry—there's plenty of time."

I didn't know if there was plenty of time or not. I marched straight up to Dad and watched him get all uncomfortable with me coming toward him. I told him about the ring before he had a chance to speak. He nodded.

The car was baking hot, but I smiled as the wind rushed against my arm hanging out the window. I waved at some of Juan Pablo's family coming in as I pulled out of the parking lot. I was free.

The wind turned to a hairdryer by the time I got out on the highway. The heat was determined to overtake me, and by the time I got to Missy's house I was almost the same color as my dress, which had turned dark where sweat poured down under my arms, all along my back, and under my boobs. I found the ring easy enough, sitting on top of Missy's dresser, a mess of hair ties and jewelry scattered around it. It was the same dresser she'd always had when we were kids, and now a wedding ring was sitting on top of it.

I went to her bathroom and tried to dry off the sweat marks with a towel. The towel turned hot pink, but the dark spots remained. I looked at myself in the mirror—red, sweaty, freckles poking through. How could I ever think someone like Sam would want me? Well, at least I had Mom's pretty hair. My eyes began to burn. It was so hot. I shoved my head under the faucet and turned on the cold water, soaking my face and neck. A pair of scissors lay on the counter. I stared at them. Then I grabbed them and cut. My hair fell in thick, long chunks.

The ring was so big. It was hard to imagine Juan Pablo had hands that big—they had to be the size of a grown man's. I slipped it on my thumb and headed back. By the time I got there everyone was inside. I snuck in the back door and ran smack into Sandy.

She looked at me and raised her eyebrows, "Oh, sweetie," she sighed. Then she started laughing—hard. "You can't get up in front of everyone looking like that," she said. "Come on."

We went into the bathroom and Sandy instructed me to take the dress off. She put the entire thing in the sink and soaked it through and through with cold water while I attempted to wipe pink dye off my armpits.

"There," she said. "You may be soaking wet, but at least your dress will be one color and we won't be staring at your pit stains."

"Thank you, Sandy. For everything."

"You are welcome," she said, sticking bobby pins between her teeth and pinning short tufts of my hair back.

Missy was calm and ready, waiting at the back of the church to walk down the aisle in rhinestone flip flops. I took my flowers, ring on my thumb, and walked down before her. The sanctuary was heavy with the smell of sweat and loud with the roar of all the fans. It was bearable when the air from the fans hit me, but when they oscillated away my skin felt like it was burning. The flowers were beautiful, and the pews were packed with Catholics. Juan Pablo stood at the front with his best friend, Marc, and my dad. He looked terrified—and happy. It was the most real play wedding Missy and I had ever had.

When I got to the front Missy walked down and everyone stood up. I knew she loved that. She had a smile on her face the whole way down the aisle, looking at Juan Pablo. The ruffles, her veil—everything blew like feathers in the breeze, except her hair, which was tacked up with a tiny tiara. She looked like an exotic bird with her protruding belly leading the way.

"The scripture tells us," Dad began, "*When I was a child, I spoke like a child, I thought like a child, I reasoned like a child; when I became an adult, I put an end to childish ways.* This ceremony signals that moment for you two, Missy and JP. It's okay to be afraid. But you are not alone in this endeavor—God is with you." He said that last part louder than usual, and he looked straight at Mom. "*Now I know only in part; then I will know fully, even as I have been fully known. And now faith, hope, and love abide, these three; and the greatest of these is love.*" Then he nodded at me.

That was my cue to go sing. I walked up the small steps to the piano with some difficulty because the inner layer of the dress was clinging to my thighs. The dress felt like it was growing heavier and wetter with each step. But it was time for the Lord's Prayer.

I began, "*Our Father, which art in heaven, hallowed be thy name.*" Then I noticed it: the dripping. Water was finding its way down the ravines of my legs and trickling toward my ankles. I looked at Mrs. Carlson on the piano and tried to speed up the song. "*Thy kingdom come, Thy will be done—*" water ran down my underarms now as well. People in the congregation began to look at each other sideways. I was suddenly struck with the image of the dress soaking in its blood-colored dye bath "*—in earth, as it is in heaven.*" It was streaming down my shins now and dripping off my elbows. "*Give us this day* *our daily bread. And forgive us our debts—*" I looked down to see if Missy noticed, but she didn't. She smiled sweetly, as if she'd rehearsed it, looking at me but not really seeing me "—*as we forgive our debtors.*" I heard murmurs then, and Dad looked around, wondering what was going on. "*Lead us not into temptation—*" he turned around and jumped. That's when I knew it must be really bad "*—but deliver us from evil: for thine is the kingdom—*" Dad opened his mouth, like he was trying to say something but didn't know what "*—and the power—*" I looked out at the crowd, searching for a friendly face, maybe even Mom "*—and the glory—*" but all I saw were the shocked faces of Juan Pablo's family. Some of them were crossing themselves and praying; others just had their faces pulled back in disgust, but they were still looking on, like a car crash "*—forever. Amen.*"

"Go wash yourself," Dad whispered angrily, as if I had purposefully appeared as a blood-soaked demon from hell just to annoy him. He turned to the pulpit, "*If I have all faith, so as to remove mountains, but do not have love, I am nothing...*"

I raced to the sink and rubbed a paper towel up and down my arms and legs and inside my thighs. I got back just in time to deliver the ring. Instead of rubbing the dye off, it had just sort of soaked into my skin and turned an unnatural fluorescent color. Missy still didn't notice. I wondered vaguely if it would ever wear off or if I would be stuck this color for the rest of my life.

"I now pronounce you husband and wife!" Dad exclaimed.

The congregation let out a relieved cheer, Missy's dad most of all.

"Oh my God! I'm so grown up now!" Missy said as she passed by me. "I'm just kidding! But seriously, I need help lifting this dress up to pee—C'mon, Jesse."

8

MUSIC AND HEAT HARMONIZED IN MY BODY

"Oh, sweetie!" Sandy jumped up from the kitchen table when I walked through the door to her condo. She had left the church right after the ceremony. I had held Missy's ruffles over the toilet about a hundred times. I had endured the uncomfortable stares of church members.

"Too bad she's not a looker like her mom," I heard an older man say to his friend when I passed by, carrying presents out to Juan Pablo's truck. I had even listened patiently to unsolicited advice from an elderly lady about how to take care of myself during my "unclean" times. I was ready to crash on Sandy's couch and forget the humiliation of the day.

"I am so sorry, Jesse. That was my fault. I shouldn't have soaked your dress," Sandy said. "You sang beautifully anyway."

"It's okay." I shrugged, thinking about Missy clambering her way into Juan Pablo's pickup—him shoving her in like a guy trying to shove a stubborn horse into a trailer. He's going to have a hard time carrying her across the threshold. They were on their way to a hotel in Fort Scott.

"Your hair looks cute," Sandy said over her shoulder, sounding casual. I did not want to talk about the symbolism of my haircut.

"Don't forget," Bonita spoke slowly, without looking up from her papers spread out on the table. "Pride is a renewable resource."

I piled up the pink ruffles in the corner of the living room that already housed my duffel bag of stuff and headed to the shower.

"Tea after I take a shower?" I asked Sandy.

"Surely."

Sandy had made lasagna with an extra layer of cheese meant to console wounded dignity. Bonita brought me some earthy smelling salt scrub that she thought might help get the pink out of my skin.

"When I was a dancer, I sometimes had to wear stage makeup—terrible stuff. I always used this scrub to get it off my face," she offered.

After dinner I sat on the couch, petting a cat, which did make me feel more like a decent human being; smelling like cloves, which did make me feel cleaner; belly full of lasagna, which did somehow make my self feel more wholesome. At least a bit.

Sandy sneezed when she came near me, opened up the cabinet under the record player and revealed two shelves of records. "Why don't you have a look, Jesse, and decide what you want to listen to."

I spent the rest of the evening laying on the floor on my stomach, pouring over the records, trying out as many as I could, and getting lost in the artwork on the covers. A cat came and snuggled into the small of my back, Sandy sometimes burst into singing along as she puttered around.

Sleep came quick but violent. Twice I shook myself awake

with gasps, dreaming of Missy's baby dropping out of her and onto its head on the wooden steps in the middle of the ceremony, dreams of me being the one with a baby coming through my thighs, blood gushing down my legs and Mom and Dad and Sam all laughing while my blood flowed down the steps of the church.

Finally, I settled into the deep sleep trench dredged by Sandy's tea and slept a dreamless sleep until dawn. Somewhere far, far away, near the surface, the front door rattled. A clumsy key, or it could have been the sound of a lock being picked, pulled me up out of the sleep trench but not out of the sea of the couch. Suddenly, I was jolted awake by the weight of someone jumping on me. Disoriented, I grunted as what felt like knees dug into my stomach. Elbows and hands clambered around the couch and my body, searching for sense in the barely lit room. It was a man. His full weight was on me, and I couldn't get up. I cried out silently a few times until I found my voice and screamed as loud as I could. A few seconds later the lights shot on, and I found myself staring into a bloody and bruised face. He shielded his eyes from the light with hands caked with dried blood and engine oil. I screamed again, even harder, and kicked him as hard as I could. He fell with a thump to the floor and groaned. Sandy ran to him.

"Cody!"

She knelt down beside him and tenderly cupped his dirty face in her hands. She took a long, silent moment then leaned her forehead against his, smearing blood on her face. My body shook.

"It's okay, sweetie," Sandy whispered. "You gonna make it?" she asked. The man nodded. "Broken bones?" The man shook his head, then flinched as Sandy lifted him upright. "Maybe," she said. He nodded again. I could see then that he wasn't a man; he was a teenager, maybe around my age. He looked up at me. His eyes sparkled like Sandy's, even in the confusion and pain, but where Sandy's were comforting, his looked dangerous.

"Should I call 911, dear?" Bonita called from the hallway.

The teenager looked up wide-eyed at Sandy.

"No," Sandy called back. "I'll get him cleaned up here." She began to help him up. "Up on the couch, sweetie." I jumped up and stood in the corner next to my ruffles. Sandy suddenly remembered I was there. "You must have gotten quite a scare, sweetie. You okay? This is my nephew, Cody. Cody, this is Jesse."

She disappeared to grab her nursing bag, and Cody looked up at me under a lowered brow. He held out his hand. I stood, frozen, staring at his bloody hand in disgust. He looked me in the eyes for a moment then let them wander down the rest of my body. I became conscious that I was only wearing my underpants and sleep tank, and that my skin was still hot pink. I reached out quickly to shake his hand.

"Sorry," he mumbled. "Didn't know you were here." His eyes turned tender, and I felt the nervousness pour out of my body.

"I," I stumbled, "it's okay," I whispered. I took back my hand. "I gotta get dressed."

Sandy whirled back to the couch with first aid supplies and wash cloths. "Jesse, why don't you make us some tea," she said.

"Sure," I mumbled, pulling my jean shorts and T-shirt on in the kitchen. I blinked in the newly orange light of sunrise. "Um, awake tea or sleep tea?" I asked.

Sandy looked Cody up and down. "Sleep tea," she decided.

I tried to make the tea the way I had watched Sandy do it. I filled a kettle with water and set it to boil on the stovetop, then reached into a tin can that set on the counter and scooped a couple spoonfuls of dried herbs into the teapot. I stared over the counter at the new person on the couch while I waited for the water to boil. The air was perfectly still, the way it is only at the first break of dawn. The only sound was the water gently bubbling. I took the dish towel, grabbed the kettle, and poured it over the herbs into the teapot. A sweet, earthy smell drifted up with the steam. I let it steep while Sandy inspected Cody for broken bones. Then I took a cup out and handed it to him. He took it with a nod, and Sandy looked at me.

"Oh, sweetie," she said, "go wash your face."

I blinked and walked to the bathroom where I saw that my face was streaked with Cody's blood. I scrubbed it with cold water. When I walked out of the bathroom, Cody was in the hall, waiting to go in and take a shower. "Sorry," I mumbled and squeezed past him.

Sandy cleaned up bloody cloths and laid a blanket out on the couch for Cody when he got out of the shower.

"I'm—I'll go home now," I said. I didn't want to go home. I still had at least fifty records to listen to, not to mention the bare walls and disinfected smell of home didn't feel like home.

Sandy stopped working and set her hand on my shoulder. "You can still sleep here, sweetie. We'll figure something out. Once we know what happened with Cody." She was distracted. She glanced over at the bathroom door and sighed. "He's a good boy. He's..." she trailed off. "Just better check and make sure it's still okay with your folks."

For the second Sunday in my life, I didn't go to church. Instead, I went to read Mr. Billy's book to the barn.

O you singer, solitary, singing by yourself—projecting me;
O solitary me, listening—nevermore shall I cease perpetuating you;
Never more shall I escape, never more the reverberations,
Never more the cries of unsatisfied love be absent from me.

When I was done I walked up to the back door and looked in at the kitchen table through the screen. A plate of cornbread was on it. My favorite. I wondered how long it had been sitting there waiting for me.

I had spent so much of my life sitting at that table wishing I was different. More like Mom. Prettier. More likeable. Living somewhere else. Trying to live up to a standard I couldn't recognize even one part of in myself. *Maybe I already know as much as her*, I thought. *Maybe I know something that's just for me to know.* I walked in and let the door slam. Mom ran from the living room to hug me.

"Jesse–" She buried her face in my neck and squeezed hard.

I hugged her back, then pulled away. "I'm done trying to be like you, Mom. I'm not the child I was before. I don't know who I am."

"I–" she stammered, "I'm just so glad you're home." Tears filled her eyes.

"I don't think I am," I said.

Her brow furrowed with worry.

Dad walked in and stared for a moment. "You're back?" he asked.

"Not yet," I answered.

Mom started to cry.

"What's in your hands there?" he said.

"It's a book. A gift. One of Sandy's patients gave it to me."

"A book?" His eyes narrowed. "What kind of book?"

"Poetry."

"Poetry?" His eyes widened. "Poetry about what?"

I popped a cornbread muffin in my mouth, then walked toward the door. "Death. I think."

"Now, wait just a minute–" Dad reeled around behind me and I closed my eyes, bracing for the deluge.

"Let her go." Mom cut him off. "Let her go."

Sandy's condo was even more fragrant than usual. I think it was jazz–blasted from the speakers. Bonita was in the kitchen, chopping onions. Sandy was next to her, flitting from fridge to counter to stovetop, humming. It smelled like all the spices mixed together. Cody sat at the table and peeled a potato. It was the first time I saw him in the full light. His left eye was bruised, and there was a bandage over his cheek bone. Another bandage stuck diagonally across his forehead. He looked up at me briefly, then returned to peeling.

"I'll do that," I sat down across from him and reached for the peeler.

"Why?" he said.

"Well, you're hurt," I mumbled. "Maybe you should rest or something."

"Working makes a body feel better," Sandy said, floating into the dining area. "Here, Jesse, you can chop the carrots." She set down a colander of carrots in front of me with a plate and knife.

"Speaking of working," I said, "can I still have that internship?"

"It's all yours. Decided to stay?" she asked, returning to the kitchen.

"If that's okay," I said.

"Okay with your folks?"

"With Mom," I said. "I just..." I glanced around the room, "I feel more comfortable here."

Cody half smiled at his potato.

"I'll sleep on the floor," I added.

"I'll take the floor," Cody mumbled.

"But–you're injured," I blurted, still not knowing what had happened to him.

"Yeah?" he said slowly.

"It isn't right for you to sleep on the floor. I'll be fine," I said. "I'm tough."

Cody stopped peeling and looked at me for a long minute. "Right," he said. "I'll take the floor."

A striped cat jumped into Cody's lap, and he set the potato down to pet it. It nestled down into him and purred. Sandy sneezed.

"Put the cat outside, dear," Bonita said.

"It's too hot," Sandy said, "I'm not going to have them die out there in the heat."

"You would have yourself die in here instead? Of course you would. She's allergic, you know," Bonita said. "Five cats and she's allergic."

"It's not like I go looking for them. They just show up here." Sandy motioned toward the table. Cody and I looked at each other, not sure if she was talking about the cats, or us.

Later that night, as spices and tea mingled in my body and words and silence mingled in the air above the couch, I laid awake, trying to fight sleep, watching the motionless figure of Cody on the floor not ten feet away. Sandy had rearranged the coffee table so he had a little nook between the table and wall. His breathing was not yet heavy, so I figured he was awake too. I smiled a little, knowing Dad would completely freak out if he knew Cody was there. Then I drifted off to sleep.

Monday morning, we left Cody sleeping soundly and went to work. I was thankful to have the internship to busy my mind. Sandy slipped another mix CD in the stereo and we moved down the highway toward my house. But before we got too far, we turned down a dirt road. After about twenty minutes of bumpy gravel, we arrived at a house. It was a tidy, little farmhouse with a neatly tended rock garden outside.

"This place looks nice," I said.

"Appearances can be deceiving," Sandy warned. She knocked loudly on the door, and we were welcomed in by a short, wide woman with an awkward smile and lemonade. A small, yapping dog ran out at us and began alternately growling and jumping on our legs.

"Zeus! Down!" the woman's voice seemed too loud for her size. "Down, Zeus! Oh, he's just excited to see you," she said, picking up the dog that was still growling at me. "Come here, my little baby," her tone turned from drill sergeant to baby talk as she nuzzled her nose into the dog's head and pulled a piece of bacon from her pocket. "Here you go, my sweet little furry one." The dog gobbled up the bacon so fast it nipped her fingers. She yanked her hand away and led Sandy and me into a bedroom down the hall. A weird, unpleasant smell wafted from the room, and I wondered what it could be coming from.

"Hello, Mr. Thomas," Sandy said brightly to a man who was lying in a bed, pillows propping him upright, face directed squarely at a TV on the dresser in front of him. The man didn't respond.

"Oh, he's just watching his program. Ted! Ted!" the woman shouted at the man just like she had at the dog. I jumped. "The nurse is here, Ted!" She reached into her pocket and pulled out another piece of bacon. I thought for a minute she was going to offer it to Ted to get his attention, but she fed it to the dog.

"I'm going to check your vitals, Mr. Thomas," Sandy said sweetly, motioning me to join her. She handed me the tablet and told me which form I needed to fill out. Blood pressure. Heart rate. Oxygen level. "Let's get you up and on the scale, Mr. Thomas," she said, then instructed me to go see if there were any dishes in the sink that needed to be cleaned.

I watched Sandy move the covers off Ted, revealing a sickening-looking leg, blotched with blue and red spots. The stench that accompanied Sandy's movement of the sheets was unbearable. I hurried out of there and to the kitchen; Ted never took his eyes off the TV.

"Zeus!" the woman shouted as I entered the kitchen, and I jumped again.

I welcomed the smell of bacon. Zeus clawed his way up my leg, and I worried that he would tear Mom's skirt. Thin, red welts started to appear on my shins from his tiny claws.

"Zeus!" she shouted again. She threw pieces of bacon on the floor to distract him.

"Do you have any dishes I can clean?" I asked.

"No. I do the dishes. *I'm* perfectly healthy."

"Oh, I didn't mean—"

"Zeus! Down!" More bacon got shoved into the fat, little dog's mouth. "It's not easy, you know."

I wasn't sure if she was talking to me or Zeus.

"He used to be real useful. He used to help out around here. Shoveled snow in winter. Went to work like a normal, respectable person, you know? But now—Zeus! Now, all he does is lay there. But at least I have you, don't I, my sweet little furry friend? Thought I'd be able to relax in my retirement. Ha! I've never worked so hard. Did you see that walkway on your way in? Every stone was laid by me. I moved every stone around this place." She gestured widely, indicating the exterior of the house. Zeus licked her face, and I tried not to show my disgust at the bacon grease being transferred from the dog's mouth to hers. "You never know when you get married. You're young—you think you'll fall in love and live happily ever after. Careful who you marry. Just make sure you get a good dog."

I decided for the third time that summer that I was never getting married. I wasn't sure what was worse: listening to this woman or watching Sandy change the bedclothes of the man in the other room. I opted for the woman, but Sandy couldn't have come out soon enough.

I practically ran out of the house and into the stifling heat. Sandy and I sat in her car, air conditioning blaring, and she told me what to type on the forms.

"Sandy," I asked, looking up, "what's wrong with him?"

"Oh, he's got a list of things wrong with him physically. But the biggest problem is his depression."

"His wife seemed so—I don't know—almost mean about it."

"His wife has been dealing with his depression for decades," she sighed. "It's not easy on either one of them. She's not the friendliest, I'll give you that. But—we never know what goes on between two people when no one else is around. I always try to give everyone the benefit of the doubt."

Sandy started down the road again. I held my breath as we passed by Dad's church, rock music pouring out the car speakers.

The next visit was a mobile home like Mr. Billy's. But I could tell from Sandy's long sigh when we pulled up the dirt drive that it wasn't going to be the same. The road was rutted out with potholes and weeds.

"It don't look like nobody drives here," I said.

"It *doesn't* look like *any*body drives here," she said. "Your mother will kill me if you go home talking like that. Take care in here, Jesse," she said. "I mean," she sighed again, "this is a tough one."

She grabbed her purse out of the back seat and didn't wait for me to get out of the car, just marched up to the door. A man greeted her. He was skinny—too skinny—and greasy. I swallowed hard thinking what the smell of this place would be. Sandy said something I couldn't hear before I got up next to them. He spotted me and interrupted her.

"Who's this you got comin' here? What is this?" His voice was raised, and his mouth was turned down so that his words came out long and drawn out.

Sandy stood right in the doorway, in between the man and me, and didn't budge even though he was pressing up against her to get a look at me. "This is our intern, Floyd, she's working with me. Now, never mind her—where's Kim?"

"Awww, she sleepin'. You come at a bad time, nurse lady," he said the word *nurse* like it was a swear word. "She *all* the way in dreamland by now." Floyd tossed his head back and laughed with a snort as he said this. He was missing most of his teeth.

"What's she on, Floyd?" Sandy demanded. "What did she take?"

"Nothin'," he shrugged his shoulders and dipped his head out and back like a weird bird. "She just knocked up again," he said.

"What?" Sandy hissed.

She pushed her way through the door, and Floyd stumbled in after her. I didn't want to go in, but I figured it was part of my job. I thought I ought to, so I stepped just inside the doorway and waited. I was right about the stench—I couldn't place the smell, or mixture of smells, but it was so awful I turned my head toward the open door to get a whiff of fresh air. Sandy had run around the back corner to the bedroom, with Floyd after her. I could hear his loud, grainy voice protesting whatever she was saying.

"Naw! Everything's fine. This ain't none o' your business—or her daddy's."

The TV was on—some old western. It was a shootout. The gunfire mixed with Sandy's firm commands, Floyd's drawled-out objections, and then a female voice, soft and whiny. I tried to make out what they were saying, but the western drowned them out. A cowboy fell from a second-story balcony. The villain mounted his horse. Sandy whipped around the corner, clutching her purse anxiously to her chest. I hurried out the door right in front of her. She stopped just at the threshold and snapped at the man.

"I'll be back, Floyd. And I'm bringing her father with me next time."

Sandy sped down the drive until we were on the main

road, then pulled over on the shoulder and tossed her purse in the back seat.

"I'm sorry about that, sweetie," she turned and looked at me, breathing deep to calm herself. "Floyd is a drug addict. You never quite know what you're walking into there. I probably should have had you stay in the car."

"That's okay," I said.

"And Kim," Sandy shook her head. "She's developmentally disabled. It was her father who hired me to come look after her. She shouldn't be living here—not with him." Sandy sighed. "Already two kids in protective services. One's blind, the other—God knows. And now she's pregnant again." She paused. "We have to get her out of there. This is the really hard part of the job, Jesse—people's choices. We can't make her leave. She has to decide to do it on her own. It's unbearable."

The day went on like that. House after house all leaving me dizzy and confused. Small, dark, cluttered homes, all with a different, nauseating stench. My eyes would adjust to the darkness inside, then I'd step back out into the blaze of midday, blinking away the sting of the sun. We'd sit down and relax as the air conditioning in Sandy's Ford slowly brought us back to life, rock music blaring, only to have it cool us too far—to the point of freezing. But we didn't care because we knew that in a few moments' time we'd be back out in the heat, opening the beige doors into a curtain of burning humidity. It took your breath away, the heat. My body felt twisted. Too much contracting and expanding with the freeze-thaw cycle. Each song that poured out of Sandy's speakers was something new and different from the one before. My head spun from the storm on my senses. Heat, cold, sounds, smells—terrible smells. I never appreciated my mom's rose candles or lavender soaps before that day. I tilted my head back against the seat, unable to take on any more sensations.

Sandy pulled back onto the main road and started back

toward her office. “Are we done now?” I asked. I wanted to take a shower—and a bath after that. I wanted to smell Mom’s lavender soap and see her soft smile. But only for a second—until I remembered.

“We’re done,” Sandy chirped. She turned off her mix CD and turned on the classical station—Chopin, “Nocturne in E-Flat Major.” I closed my eyes and thanked God for the familiar sound of the soft piano.

9

NINE MONTHS

The next morning I awoke foggy eyed, stretching and yawning, then remembered Cody was a few feet away and sat up to look at him. He was already awake, and the sleeping bag was rolled up and shoved under the side table. The smell of coffee filled the room, and I turned to find Cody sitting at the table with a cup of coffee and an *Autotrader* magazine.

"Oh, good, you're awake." Sandy pulled bread and butter out of the cabinets for breakfast. "Jam or peanut butter, sweetie?"

"Peanut butter–Jam," Cody and I answered at the same time.

"Thank you," I said.

"Sweetie, would you do me a favor and take Cody to the auto parts store this morning? I can go visit the first couple patients here in town without you, and then I'll pick you up back here and we can head out to your neck of the woods." She set toast, peanut butter, and jam in the center of the table.

"Sure," I said.

"More coffee, dear?" she asked Cody.

"Thanks," he said and handed Sandy his cup.

"You drink coffee?" I asked.

"I drink what's there to drink," he answered, looking at his magazine and flipping a page. This time a gray cat sat on his lap.

We finished breakfast listening to Sandy tell us about Parkinson's disease and what a nice lady she was going to take care of that morning, in between all her sneezing and nose blowing.

Cody followed me out the door and climbed on in the passenger seat of the Buick. He didn't ask if I was old enough to drive, he just got in.

It was a short ride to the auto parts store, but it felt longer.

"So, you were in a car accident?" I asked, hoping to get some explanation.

"Not really. Well, sort of," he said. He crossed his arms and looked up at the roof of the car, which was touching the top of his head.

"I gotta stop for gas," I said.

The station was the only one around for miles, and it had a little tourist shop in it. The sign read, *Real Indian Artifacts—Cowboy Saloon—Old West Souvenirs.* I wondered what someone from California would think of it.

We pulled up behind a car that had one of those *Native* bumper stickers—the ones where it looks like the tags from their state but instead of numbers and letters it says "Native" on it.

We watched the driver fill his tank up while we waited for our turn. He was an older, white man wearing a baseball cap and a Rockies T-shirt. He polished the rear lights of an already shiny truck while he waited.

I nodded toward the bumper sticker. "Does that make you mad?" I asked. Cody shrugged his shoulders and shrank down a little lower into the seat. We rode the rest of the way in silence.

I followed Cody around the auto parts store, feeling like a lost puppy. Some parts he picked up right away without a glance, others he studied for what seemed like an hour before adding them to the cart. I fiddled with tools I didn't know the names of, felt all the different kinds of tread on the tires, and tousled the fuzzy dice.

"You really know what you're doing, don't you?" I asked, breaking the silence.

Cody shrugged. "It's what I do," he said.

"Fix cars?"

"Yeah."

"Is that your job?"

"More like a hobby, but it'll probably be my job someday."

It was the most words I'd heard him say altogether. The guy at the checkout eyed Cody suspiciously. He kept looking at me.

"You okay?" he asked me.

"Fine, thanks, and you?" I answered and helped bag the stuff Cody bought.

When we finally got back to Sandy's she was there, waiting for me to head out to Mr. Billy's house. "Didn't want to leave without you," she said. "Mr. Billy would be disappointed—he likes you."

"He does? How can you tell?"

"I can always tell," she said, glancing at Cody.

He disappeared with his box of parts to the far side of the parking lot without a word.

I slid into Sandy's car, relieved to be in the air conditioning again.

"Mix CD?" I asked with a smile.

Mr. Billy was in the same position we left him in before—I mean the *exact* same position. My theory that he was a statue solidified.

"I read your book," I said as Sandy whisked away to the kitchen.

"Your book. I gave it to you," Mr. Billy shot words at me.

"Oh, well I read it. I read it out loud. Outside, just like you said." He didn't say anything. I thought about what Sandy said last time about me doing the nursing by talking to him about something he liked. "I think it's about death." I swallowed. "And listening. But I think it's really about figuring out who you are and what you want to say—even in the middle of sadness and loss and change. And maybe even...even because of it?"

A light seemed to shine from behind Mr. Billy's good eye, and it looked bluer somehow. He almost smiled. His voice was soft and gruff. "Well, little darling," he said. I grinned. "Sandy!" he shouted toward the kitchen. "Found a good one, here." But he didn't take his eye off me.

"Well, I know that, Mr. Billy. Why'd you think I brought her along?"

"Here!" I jumped as he pushed another book at me. "Here's another one." I took it. "This here's hard to figure out. But there's one," *breath* "*perfect* line in it. Perfect. The poet took nine months to pick out," *breath* "one word. Can you imagine that? Now, little darlin', you read this one, and see if you can find out," *breath* "which word it is."

"I'm worried about you, Mr. Billy," Sandy called from the kitchen. "I mean with this heat."

"Don't worry about an old man," he grumbled.

"I'm not worried about some old man. I'm worried about *you*. What are you doing to stay cool in here?"

"Been through droughts before," he said. "Get through this one too."

"Well, I brought you an extra fan anyway. I'll just get it out of the car." Sandy went out to get the fan, and I looked around the room some more.

"Did you get all these turtle shells from the woods around here?" I asked.

"I did. You'd be amazed what you can find. If you take the time to stop and look," he said.

"The woods here are a little different than the ones out by my house," I said. "The best thing I ever found was a snakeskin."

"That's a good find," he nodded.

"Yeah, better than all the crabapples and cicada shells," I said.

He shook his head slightly. "Cicada shells make great rattles." He nodded toward a stick with cicada shells tied to it on the shelf by the window. "Magicicadas are here. You hear 'em singing. Born from an egg, reborn seventeen years later. Transformed," *breath* "into a mystical singer down in the mud. I'll take a cicada over a butterfly," *breath* "any day." I picked up the stick and shook it. "Got a whole grove of crabapple trees out there, behind the cottonwoods." He lifted his hand, motioning toward the side of the mobile home. "*Prairie fire* crabapples. Most beautiful trees in the world, come springtime." Then he leaned in closer to me with that flame back in his eye. "Tell you what, little darlin'," he said. "You come back here with Miss Sandy. Next spring. See for yourself. The entire forest looks like it's on fire. Blossoms red as blood."

"Here you go, handsome!" Sandy came in with the fan. "I'm going to plug it in over here, and hopefully combined with the other one you can get a cross breeze in here." She went over to the far wall, hunting for an outlet.

"Thank you," I leaned in close and spoke to Mr. Billy. He looked pleased as punch. "Thank you for the book. I'll look real hard for that word."

"You do that, little darlin'. You do that."

In the car with Sandy on our way to Zeus's house I couldn't stop thinking about what Mr. Billy said.

"How could someone take nine months to think up of a

word?" I asked, flipping through the book.

"I'm no writer, but I can imagine he was searching for just the right one," Sandy said.

"Yeah, but *nine* months? You could read through the entire dictionary in shorter time than that and pick any word in the whole world!"

"That poem was his creation, Jesse. Think about if your dad only wrote one long sermon for his whole life's work. Wouldn't he take nine months to make sure everyone who heard it would be moved by his words?"

"I suppose. But my dad would never sit still just to think."

"How about your mom? She spent nine months creating you."

I pondered that for a moment. I never thought about Mom or Dad creating me. They always said I was given to them by God.

Just then Sandy's phone rang. It was sitting in the cup holder.

"It's my mom," I said.

"Well, pick it up—you gotta start somewhere."

I turned the rock music off and answered the phone. Mom had news about Missy. She was waiting tables at the restaurant when her water broke, right there under a tray of burritos, right in front of a booth full of people. According to the hostess who called Mom, Missy set the tray down calmly, walked back to the kitchen, and started to scream. It was five weeks early, but with the heat and working all day on her feet like that, no one was surprised. Mom said I should head down to the hospital as soon as I could.

Sandy and I went ahead and visited the next patients, Zeus and Ted. The TV was turned on to the same program as last time, and the horrible smell of sickness mixed with bacon still lingered in the air. This time I came equipped with a spade and a determination to stay outdoors and pull dandelions out of the rock garden. Even the heat of the afternoon was better than listening to that woman yell at Zeus, or Zeus devour that bacon. I dug the spade under the yellow flowers and Sam was there—in my mind's eye. The last time I'd pulled weeds. Sam scrawling something in his notebook. Asking me if I ever thought about leaving. But here I was, still in Bourbon County, still pulling weeds. And he was off seeing the world some more. Sandy assumed when she came out and found me crying, I was worried about Missy. I didn't correct her. She drove me to Fort Scott and dropped me off at the hospital.

I had no idea what I was supposed to do, but neither did Missy's dad, so we sat together in silence, him reading a parenting magazine and me watching Juan Pablo's family on the other side of the room. We just sat there and stared at each other. Never said a word. Missy's dad flipping pages. Juan Pablo's little sister whispering to his mom. The room was too cold with air conditioning, and too clean, and too quiet. There were no windows, no sunlight. I thought of all the families who learned they had a new person in this room. And all the ones who learned they had one less person. Babies born in the same place where people got sick and died. Like a doorway.

Missy's dad picked up a different magazine and Juan Pablo's mom gave his little sisters snacks. They laughed and chased each other around the waiting room. Then Juan Pablo's dad came in with his uncle and aunt. They smiled and joked and I wished I was sitting over there with them. Finally, Missy's mom came watery eyed, into the room. She passed by Juan Pablo's family and marched up to Missy's dad and me.

"It's a girl!" she said beaming. "She's fine. They're both fine. She's so little you can't imagine!" She looked thrilled, and I guessed the miracle of life had warmed her to Missy again. Juan Pablo's family looked over at us, anxiety and fear mixed with anticipation. But they didn't ask what happened, didn't try to overhear. Missy's dad stood up and hugged her mom.

She began to weep into his shoulder, her body shaking. He stood still and held her. Worry swept over Juan Pablo's mom's face. A few moments later Juan Pablo came into the room and said the same thing to his family, but in Spanish. They erupted in smiles and laughter. He was congratulated with pats on the back and ruffled hair. He was pale and his eyes were distant; like he'd just witnessed a terrible crime.

We weren't allowed to hold the baby because she was in an incubator on account of being born so early. But we could look at her through a window. Juan Pablo grasped her impossibly small hand like she was made of dynamite that might explode at any minute. She was incredibly small, like Missy's mom said. And all wrinkled. I couldn't imagine being in charge of keeping alive something so fragile. Missy didn't want to see anyone except Juan Pablo and her mom, so I waved to the tiny human and wandered out into the gracious night air.

10

TWISTER

It was the kind of sky that makes people believe in God. A huge ceiling of gray, with streaks of orange light breaking through—light from another world. The heavens. The light looked like Cody and I could reach out and grab it in our hands, put it in our pockets and take it home.

I was walking with Cody out to the sunflower field because in a choice between awkwardness with Cody and awkwardness with my parents, Cody won out. Sandy, Cody, and I had driven up to the farm out beyond the Richardson's property because corn was in season and because of the drought they had produced way less. Sandy wanted to go to the farmstand and make sure we got the good stuff before all the city folk bought it up and trucked it to the grocery stores.

It's true that I loved corn on the cob almost as much as I loved summer; one being indistinguishable from the other in my mind. I had won the church corn-on-the-cob eating context six years in a row and counting, and the school corn-on-the-cob eating contest, and have entertained the idea of entering the county one. I could put down corn on the cob like a plague of locusts devouring every piece and parcel of green covering the land. But the good Lord says not to brag.

We passed my house on the way to the farmstand, but as we neared it going back Sandy slowed down.

"Now don't be mad at me, Jesse," she said. "Your dad called me and said he wouldn't allow you stay at our place any longer unless you came home from time to time and started trying to work things out with your mom."

I groaned. "What—now? You lured me here with corn?!"

"It's either this, or you move back home. I don't think what your parents have done is grounds for legal separation," Sandy said.

I scowled, but she took the turn off the old highway and we jiggled over the washboards to my house. Cody said he'd stay outside and started walking along the tracks under the cottonwoods, but Sandy came in with me. Mom had cookies and sun tea around the coffee table. Just like she did for the church ladies when they came over on Thursdays. It felt weird. Mom said how happy she was I was there. To try to work it out, she said. *Work what out*, I said.

I sat, realizing as I did it that the last time I sat there Sam had barged through the door and my life had done a cartwheel. The image of Mom's pale face got stuck in my mind. Sandy was real good at talking about stuff and making things less awkward, so she started doing that while I ate cookies. About five minutes later Cody burst through the door.

"It's too hot," he said. His face was sweaty and red. Mom jumped up and got another glass for tea. Dad, in all his wisdom, brought up the sinful nature of Missy's baby. Cody sat down looking like a fox caught in a kennel. Trying to will his body to camouflage with the pea-green couch and disappear.

"Babies are a lot of work, Jesse. I hope you could see that when you saw her. I hope you can make some smarter choices now," Dad preached, eyeing me closely while he sipped his tea.

I looked at Mom, trying to read from her expression just what she had told Dad. She had promised not to tell, but now—I couldn't trust her.

Dad droned on. "Missy is going to have to overcome a lot to have a chance to succeed in this world—"

I slammed my glass down hard on the table. Mom and Cody jumped in their seats.

"I'm going for a walk," I copied Dad's slow, quiet way.

"Me too!" Cody jumped up. So much for it being too hot. I sped out the kitchen door fast enough that Mom couldn't get a word in. I had wanted to go out to the barn, but with Cody tagging along I decided to walk toward the sunflower field instead. It was in the same direction as the barn, but further west, at the base of the plateau.

We walked along in silence, past the spot where the milkweeds grow—where I first saw the butterflies. Then we walked past the spot where I kissed Sam and my stomach lurched. A criminal returning to the crime scene. The land sloped downward to the west and we followed it.

I resisted the urge to break the silence with whatever even more awkward thing might come out of my mouth. I thought for a moment Cody might understand if I told him about the monarchs. There was something about him, something in his eyes that reminded me of the brightness in Mr. Billy's good eye. You had to look close to see it and he had to want to *let* you see it. But I decided to keep quiet. Cody let his hands out of his front pockets for once and his long arms swung down. His fingers were scratched up and dirty from working on his car.

"How long've you had that car?" I asked at last.

"Five years, I guess. My uncle left it to me when he died. I was only twelve. I guess he knew it would take me that long to get it running." He half smiled like I'd seen once before.

"Oh, I'm sorry. About your uncle, I mean. Was he sick?" I

asked.

He bent his head down to its usual position and kicked at some dirt. "He knew he was going to die," he said pushing a piece of greasy hair behind his ear.

The thirsty dust under our feet gave way to tall, yellow grass as we reached the bottom of the plateau. It swept up to our calves and knees and, as we walked further, tickled my stomach. Cody let his hands brush the top of the grass, stroking it as he walked.

"So, what happened?" I asked. "To your car, I mean. Sandy said you were driving across the whole country. How'd you get all broken down out here?"

"My car didn't break down," he countered. "She's solid." Cody sighed and looked at me for a moment, like he was deciding whether or not he should tell me. When he finally spoke, there was a sadness in him that made my chest tighten. *No wonder he didn't talk more,* I thought. He stopped walking and looked at me and I began to see the ember, glowing and flickering.

"She's black with white leather interior and black accents. Beautiful. 1970 Chevelle. Driving east—it was like sailing." The half smile swept across his face. "I started right at the ocean, then crossed the Sierra Nevada's, drove into the desert." He started walking again.

"What's it like?" I interrupted. "The ocean."

He thought before he answered.

"It's really calm—and turbulent. It's powerful. When you're in it you feel it pull you. It sounds like life. I don't just mean the waves crashing on the beach and that—I mean when you're out, floating around, it sounds like...if life had a voice. And when you look at it, sometimes you think you'll never be able to look away."

I stared, wide-eyed. I couldn't move, couldn't speak. But something inside me was dancing and singing. Cody cleared his throat and kept talking.

"I drove at night through the desert. It was too hot in the day. Daytime I'd find a movie theater and nap in the air conditioning. Driving at night—it's another world. You can't imagine how many stars—I could disappear there. There's nothing ahead of you beyond what the headlights shine on. And nothing behind or on either side. Just above." Cody looked up at the sky, seeing the stars in his mind's eye.

"But even though you're driving and driving—and I mean fast—there's nobody else on the road so you can go as fast as you want—no matter how long and fast you go, the stars look the same. They don't move behind you."

"Your folks just let you go on a road trip like that—all on your own?" I asked.

"They don't really mind what I do," he shrugged. "Not the way your parents do. When I reached the Rockies, the mountains were high and rough. Where I live, things grow everywhere. It's soft, like moss. But those peaks were like spikes. I thought, *if we go over the edge we'll be stabbed*, you know? Harpooned out there, on the tip of a mountain, and no one would reach us to pull us back onto the road. Even the trees were sharp. I camped on forest access roads. Woke up sore because the ground was so hard. Rocks everywhere. My Chevelle kept going though—didn't matter how high we drove or how steep—she kept on."

Before this moment, I'd never heard Cody speak more than two sentences together. And now, his speech rose and fell like wind in the trees. I felt swallowed up in the tone of his voice.

"We made it through the mountains and reached the plains," he went on, "I never knew so much space existed on land. It was like the moon. Or a dry ocean bed. There's nothing—just nothing out here. I kinda wanted to turn back, but I wanted to see Sandy. She's, well...she lived with us for a while when I was a kid. She understands me."

Cody paused for a moment and bent his head down again, sweeping his hands across the grass and watching the dust lift up off it. Grasshoppers jumped out in front of us and I suddenly became aware of how hot I was. Sweat trickled down the back of my neck. Cody took a long breath, shoved his hands deep into his pockets and walked with his eyes focused on the ground.

"So I kept driving," his voice took on the tone of someone reading a school report. "Hoping the road would at least curve at some point. I decided to drive as long as I could and not stop to sleep—to get it over with. But at some point I got tired. Not far from here. It was the middle of the night. I pulled onto an off ramp and parked next to a field by the highway, just to sleep for a while. I had passed a hundred off ramps in Kansas and never saw anyone there. I laid down in the back seat and I guess I was more tired than I thought because I don't remember falling asleep. But I woke up to the sound of the headlights being kicked in.

"I wasn't sure if I was dreaming or not. I jumped up so fast my head hit the roof and I got out, dizzy, shouting at them to stop. But I didn't know what or who was there. I started to make them out in the dark. White guys...drunk of course, three of them. You know what the scariest thing is? Recognition. They were surprised to see me. Started talking, *How'd a wetback like you get a car like this? He must've stolen it. Only way a fucking spic could get a car like this is if he stole it.* You know—stuff like that. They were looking for a fight. Thought I was Mexican.

"So I started punching. Got a few good hits in. Took down the one closest to me for long enough to go for the other two but—three on one. No contest. They pushed me into the hood and I was like, *please, please don't hurt the car.* They started punching, but they were so drunk they were sloppy. They kicked me to the ground. One of them—the fat one—kicked me in the ribs then kneeled down on my chest while he shoved his hands in my pockets, looking for the key. I couldn't breathe. He smelled like piss and blood. Probably wasn't the first fight they'd had that night. He found the key and got up. I rolled over, tried to breathe—spit a little blood. When I started breathing, I started laughing. Couldn't help it. I fixed it so my Chevelle can't be stolen. I detach one of the wires to the ignition when I'm parked—you can't start it unless you know how to hot wire it. They would have never figured it out.

"*This fucking piece of shit!* they yelled, all pissed off. *Should've known it's such a piece of shit it won't even start!* So then they came for me. I thought that was it. They looked scared—but in the form of hate. That's the worst kind. I looked up at the stars 'cause...I wanted that to be the last thing I saw, not the stupid faces of those guys. One of them got a few good kicks in, the littlest one. *Stop fucking laughing*, he was screaming. And the stars—they looked the same as they did in the desert.

"Then a truck pulled up. Eighteen-wheeler. Shined his lights on us. He had to have known what was going on when he saw me. He stayed there—middle of the off ramp. Didn't get out, didn't move.

"All three of them turned around and headed back to their pickup. But not before giving a few more kicks to my car. They tried to tear the stereo out and kicked out the emergency break. It's all fixable stuff. I got lucky, really. When that truck pulled in."

Cody turned to look at me with what seemed like satisfaction on his face. I was thunderstruck. It was the most horrible and honest thing I'd ever heard anyone say. It was also the most swear words I'd ever heard.

"That's terrible," I said. "Cody, it's so awful. Did you call the police?"

"Jesse, you don't call the police when you look like me. That would have made it worse."

I let the horror of that sink in. "Well, did the trucker get out finally to help you? How did you get out of there?" I asked.

"The trucker sat there with his lights on until the guys drove off. Then he drove away. Down the dark road. I never saw him. I crawled in the back seat and went back to sleep."

"What? You went back to sleep?"

"I laid my coat over the upholstery so I wouldn't get blood on it."

"Are you crazy? You stayed there?"

He shrugged. "What else could I do? I still had my car. But I couldn't drive at night with no headlights."

"Well, is it, I mean, are you okay?" I stumbled.

"Sure, I'm okay. It's not the first time I've been in a fight." He kicked the dirt. "It makes me really fucking angry if that's what you mean. But we made it out okay this time, my Chevelle and me. We're okay."

"And those guys just got away with it."

Cody grunted. "People get away with stuff every day. It's the American way. You know the reason why they hate me so much–it's because they hate themselves. They were disgusting. They didn't know who I was. They hated the idea of me. They were killing me to kill part of them–the part that's scared of me. They'll never be able to get away from that."

Shame entered my body and made my stomach churn. For being white. For being from Kansas. For not understanding. It swam around my blood, looking for a place to live.

"I've never heard anybody talk like you before," I said.

He blushed and pushed his hair behind his ear.

"I'm sorry," I said. "It's a stupid thing to say. But I don't know what else to say."

He nodded.

"I guess I don't really know anything. I've lived out here

all my life." I threw my hands out in front of me. "Like you said, there's just nothing out here."

Just then we came up on the ridge and the sunflower field spilled out in front of us in all its yellow brilliance.

"Well, there's this," Cody said stopping. He gazed on the field and took his hands out of his pockets. The sunflowers were in bloom, and it looked like the sun was shining up from below. The rest of the prairie was thirsting for even one drop of rain, but the sunflowers would grow taller than me by the time they were ready for harvest, water piped in from a river in Colorado. We looked at it in silence for a few moments.

"How about you?" Cody asked. "How'd you end up all broken down at Sandy's?" I laughed. "Your dad, he's a minister, right?"

"Yeah."

"So, does that mean you, uh, you try to save people's souls and all that?"

"No. Some do, but that isn't our way."

"You like, pray all the time?"

"Not really. Well, maybe. Dad does. Mostly I just listen."

"Listen for what?" he asked. I looked at him sideways and tried to speak as honestly as he just had.

"For something in the sound the wind makes coming across the plains."

He didn't say anything and I thought I might die of embarrassment. I kicked the fractured dirt at my feet.

"Back home, when there's a heavy mist, the trees creak. I like to listen to it." He looked at me from under furrowed eyebrows, squinting the sun out, and the ember glowed brighter.

"Sandy said you have the Medicine," I said. "What does that mean?" He shrugged and looked down.

"So, your dad kicked you out?" he asked.

"I left. They lied to me about when I was born." Suddenly

it sounded like a real stupid thing to be mad about. “But actually it was my mom. She—” Now I shoved my hands in my pockets and thought about whether or not to tell him. “She had an affair with this guy I had a crush on,” I sighed. Cody raised his eyebrows and nodded slowly.

We made our way to the center of the sunflower field and were surrounded by their yellow faces. Just then a streak of sunlight hit them and they lifted up toward the sky.

“I went to church a couple times,” Cody said. “A girl convinced me to go.” He looked embarrassed. “I don’t understand how all of existence can be based on a book. I like to read, sometimes, but I’m not gonna let a book tell me what to think, how to fish, how to love.” He stopped and let his hand run over the tops of the sunflowers. “Most things you have to feel to know,” he said.

I smiled and let my hands run over the sunflowers the way he was. The petals were cool and velvety soft. “I still like books,” I said, thinking of Mr. Billy’s book.

Then, all of a sudden, the sunflowers bowed their heads. The sunlight vanished behind black clouds. Black as night.

The sky had changed as we walked along, but we hadn’t noticed. The gray ceiling had flattened into a black wall—and lightning etched its way through the darkness.

“That’s an ominous sky,” I said, stopping to look behind us.

“What’s that mean?” Cody asked.

“It means we need to head back.” The clouds began to circle high above us. I searched for a patch of blue and headed in that direction. Fast as I could. Then, in the breadth of one step, the air became still. So still I could feel the electricity and humidity close around me like a warm bath. There wasn’t one sound—not birds nor crickets nor even the wind. The hair on the back of my neck stood on end and my arms and legs erupted in goosebumps.

"That's funny," Cody said. "I've never seen the sky look green like that."

"We need to go. *Now*," I commanded.

"I'm not afraid of a storm," he said, sounding tough.

"How about a twister?"

"A what?"

"Are you afraid of a tornado? 'Cause one's coming." The wind picked up and blew my hair in front of my face. It billowed up through my shirt and twisted all around my body. If I wasn't so scared it would have felt good.

Cody stared at my shirt, blowing around, and when he noticed me looking at him, he turned away and blushed. I almost forgot we were about to be blown halfway to China when I saw Cody looking up my shirt. And I didn't know if God would pluck me up right there and toss me into the sky for entertaining the notion of a boy seeing me in my bra for the second time in as many months, but I figured God would forgive me after hearing the way Cody described the ocean. We needed to find shelter.

"We don't have time to make it home," I said. "Follow me—we can't stay out here."

I had to take him to the barn. As determined as I was to keep it a secret from everyone in the world, we didn't have a choice. The wind blew harder, so hard I wasn't sure I could keep my feet on the ground. Blackness swallowed the last shafts of light and a shadow fell on us. I steered us toward the little ravine where the barn was and we slid down the dusty hill on our heels and back sides. Dots of blood appeared on my palms where gravel scraped the skin. There was a break from the wind down in the dry creek bed and Cody thought this was where I was leading him. He hunkered down against the embankment and covered his eyes. The tall grass on the ridge above us flattened, pushed by a wall of dirt so thick it appeared solid, like a train rolling over the plain.

"C'mon!" I shouted over the wind, which was starting to sound like a giant, pounding toward us.

"There's dirt in my eyes," he hollered back.

"It doesn't matter!" I yelled. He didn't seem to understand the danger we were in. "C'mon! I don't care if you can see or not!" I shouted.

Of course the wind was blowing dirt in our eyes—and noses and ears and mouths and everywhere it could get it. The drought had turned most of the prairie into a dust pile. I pulled Cody up and dragged him by the hand down the creek path. Then it happened.

The sky opened up and it rained.

Hard. Like a giant lake dumped out on top of us.

It was like one of those midsummer, evening rains. The ones that are brought on by the heat that's been scorching the earth after a long day. The ones that sneak up on you and poor down so much water you think it's going to flood like it did for Noah, for days and days. And then, just as soon as it starts, it stops again and the ground is covered in steam. Only this time, it wasn't the heat of a long day it was quenching—it was the heat of a long summer month.

The rain stung my back and head and I lifted my arms up for cover. I saw the barn up ahead and pointed to it. Cody realized then that I was taking us somewhere inside and started running fast, toward it. Then the rain turned to hail. It tore into the earth in a relentless torrent. All those little yellow flowers were ripped apart, their mutilated petals carpeting the dirt. Milkweed hacked to pieces. Bodies of insects littering the white of the hail stones. I thought I might sob.

We were getting pelted hard. I looked toward the barn and stumbled. My legs went limp. My tree, my climbing tree was bent at an unnatural angle. One huge branch had already snapped and swung around wildly, banging into the trunk. I thought of the birds that housed there. I wanted to cry but the wind stole my breath. Like I was in one of those dreams where you need to scream but try as you might you just can't get it out.

I crouched down and tried to breathe. My chest heaved and air must have filled my lungs but I couldn't recognize it. Hail beat against my exposed neck. Cody doubled back when he noticed I wasn't still running alongside him. He took my hand and pulled me upwards and forward until we reached the barn.

"That hail is huge!" Cody said as we tucked inside the door. Welts formed on his arms.

"Yeah," I mumbled. But I wasn't paying attention to what he said. Cody was in my barn. He rubbed his eyes with the bottom of his soaked shirt then looked around, noticing all my secret things. The wind chimes blew like crazy—and the dried flowers and grass braids. All those little parts of me that I had gathered there for just me and the prairie to share. It was like he was invading my mind. I wanted him to close his eyes. To pretend not to see it.

But he kept looking around. He was noticing *everything*. And then he looked at me and nodded.

"Now I see you."

Just then the wind and hail stopped. The air froze. My heart pounded against my wet shirt. I grabbed Cody's hand and pulled him down into the northeast corner of the barn, inside a boarded-up square that used to be a feed hold for horses. "Get ready," I said. "Here it comes."

He looked at me, kind of confused. Then we heard it.

People say a tornado sounds like a freight train coming through your living room. The thing is, I have a freight train coming through my front yard, and I can tell you, it sounds way worse than that. It sounds like a freight train coming right over the top of your head. Cody grabbed me and pulled me up next to him, real tight. I was more scared than I'd ever been, but it felt great, him holding me like that. He pulled me to him like we were about to leave this earthly world and he didn't want to leave it alone.

The twister moved in close and part of the roof flew off. We looked up and saw the giant, terrible funnel on the ridge above us. I watched another branch snap off my tree and my heart snapped with it. The funnel sucked it up and devoured it. The tip of the spiral drilled into the soil and yanked it up into its grip, leaving the earth gouged and maimed in its wake. The barn trembled violently and slats on the broken-down side hurled into the sky. Bits and pieces of wind chimes fell around us.

Suddenly I scolded myself for making them out of nails. The noise was so loud it hurt my ears. I buried my head in Cody's shoulder and placed one arm around the back of my neck and threw my other arm around the back of his. He closed his face in down next to mine and put both arms around me as tight as he could. I couldn't tell if it was Cody's embrace or the twister that was sucking the air out of me.

Hay swirled with dust, and rocks bashed into the walls, splintering the wood around us. The ground shook underneath, and I opened my eyes—because I wanted my tree—or the creek bed—to be the last thing I saw. Cody pulled my head back against his shoulder, and I squeezed my eyes shut again.

Then, just like that, it was silent.

The ground was still. The air was a frozen dust cloud. We clung together. I thought I heard something far away and lifted my head. It was Cody—he was still holding me. He was talking but I couldn't hear him. Then his voice flooded into my ears and he was right there, in front of me again. It was over.

"You're hurt, Jesse," Cody said. I blinked, trying to understand him. He spoke, but the words only came to my ears half the time. I looked around.

"You've got something in your arm," I coughed.

A long splinter of wood, about half an inch thick stuck straight through his arm, in one side and out the other.

"Don't pull it out," I said, able think again. "It'll start bleeding like crazy. I saw a cow one time with a piece of straw stuck right through its leg after a tornado. Mr. Richardson pulled it out and it bled so bad he almost had to put her down."

"Well, you're bleeding like crazy right now," Cody said.

"I am?" I couldn't feel anything. Then I started laughing. I couldn't stop.

"What's so funny?" he asked. Cody stood up and briefly glanced at his arm, like he was checking the time.

"I'm just so happy that it rained," I said. I felt dizzy. "Let's go home, it's not far."

"How far?" Cody asked.

"A mile."

"That's too far, Jesse. You stay here and I'll go get someone." I tried to get up, but the barn, or what was left of it, started spinning around me. For a moment I thought we were in the funnel. Cody squeezed my shoulders and set me back down. He looked around the ground and picked up one of my grass braids.

"Sit right there. Don't move your head. At all. Sit there and fix this." He handed me the braid. I stared wide-eyed at the wood sticking through his arm. "What direction do I walk to get to your house?" he asked.

"Just follow the creek south. It's just right up that way," I waved my hand in the general direction.

"No, seriously don't move," he said, gently pushing my arm back down. Then he ran out toward the creek.

It felt like he was only gone for about a minute, but then it felt like he was gone for a day, too. I did what I was told and re-braided the grass he had handed me, then wondered what on earth I was doing at a time like this. I reached down to set the braid by my feet and noticed my shirt was soaked with blood. It ran from my shoulder down my breasts. *Mom's gonna kill me*, I thought. *This is her blouse.*

My ears began ringing and I felt like lying down real bad, but I remembered what Cody said. I tried to think of something to distract me from moving.

"Who has cut a channel for the torrents of rain," I recited out loud, *"and a way for the thunderbolt, to bring rain on a land where no one lives, on the desert, which is empty of human life, to satisfy the waste and desolate land—"* I took a breath. *"The sniff of green leaves and dry leaves...and of hay in the barn, the sound of the belch'd words of my voice loos'd to the eddies of the wind, a few light kisses, a few embraces, a reaching around of arms, the play of shine and shade on the trees as the supple boughs wag..."*

My head thumped against the shattered wood behind it, I closed my eyes, and everything went mute and red.

11

A NEW LANGUAGE

"You had a *rusty nail* lodged in your ear." I heard Dad's voice, but I couldn't see him. My eyes wouldn't open. He said the words *rusty nail* like they were swear words he was forced to repeat against his will. "Had us worried sick." Something was on my face, I reached up my hands and felt tubes coming out of my nose. "I don't—what you even—*think*." Half of my head was numb, including my face. I forced the un-numb eye open. "Wandering out—with that *boy*." Dad was fuzzy. Sitting next to me. We were in a hospital. "Doing God knows—death trap of a barn." A machine beeped somewhere in the distance. "Accident waiting to happen."

"Are you talking to me," I tried to say, but it came out like a toad croaking. He came into focus. It looked like he'd been crying, but since that's how he always looked I couldn't tell if it was on account of my situation or not.

"You're lucky that nail didn't reach your brain," he said. Was he sure it hadn't? 'Cause it sure felt there might be a rusty nail in my brain. "That boy is lucky too. A piece of wood went straight through his arm. He's lucky it wasn't some other part of his *body*." The word *body* came out like a swear. Why was

Dad swearing so much?

A flash of light snapped into my eyes—the funnel cloud. Cody's arms around my body. My bent and broken tree.

A nurse showed up and pushed a button on a beeping machine, then changed a bandage on my ear, and one on my back.

"You're a very lucky young lady," she said. "Something cut a deep gash back here—a couple centimeters further and it would have impaled your lung. Maybe even your heart. You've got stitches back there now. They'll dissolve in a couple weeks."

Maybe even my heart? A deep gash on the back side of my lung. That's where Cody's arm was. The one with the wood straight through it.

That's where he saved my life.

Dad stood up and looked at me like I was an alien. "Why are you smiling?" he fumed, nostrils flared.

"I guess 'cause I'm so lucky," I coughed.

"Your mother will be here shortly," he said, turning to go.

"You're leaving?" I asked.

"I have work to do. One of the families in our congregation needs counseling."

"But—I'm in a hospital," I mumbled. "Got a nail in my ear. Rusty one." But he didn't hear me, he was already out the door.

Mom came and went and came and went so often I started to ignore her. I could see from her face she'd been crying. But every time her eyes welled up she rushed out into the hallway. Sandy stopped by and brought me the new book Mr. Billy had given me.

"Honestly, Jesse," Sandy said, "when you saw those clouds, why didn't you come back inside?"

"I wasn't paying attention," I said. "I was listening to Cody—he told me what happened."

She sighed.

I guess Mr. Billy thought I had nothing but time on my hands to look up every other word in the poem he had given me. But it turns out he was right. I sat in the hospital bed for two days and three nights and looked up the words about ten times each.

At first the poem was too hard to understand and I gave up, but boredom drove me to look at it again. After a while I started to love it—even if I didn't know what it meant.

Of rimless floods, unfettered leewardings—

Unfettered: to free from restraint; liberate.

Leeward: the point toward which the wind blows.

Laughing the wrapt inflections of our love;
Take this Sea, whose diapason knells
On scrolls of silver snowy sentences—

Diapason: a full, rich outpouring of melodious sound.

Knells: the sound announcing the death of a person.

All but the pieties of lovers' hands...
Adagios of islands, O my Prodigal,
Complete the dark confessions her veins spell.

I knew all about the prodigal son and confessions. There was even one part of the Bible that mentioned kisses and perfume, but the pieties of lovers' hands perplexed me. As I read the poem over again, the book I had known my whole life, the only book I'd known, became a mystery to me. Its familiar words gave themselves over to me in a foreign way. Here was a whole new language—it was English, but it tilted and pulsed and rose and fell in complete dissonance with my own English and the English my father spoke at the pulpit. I read it out loud because I was sure that's what Mr. Billy would want. After a day, my head started burning from the feeling of it in my mouth. The nurses gave me pills to bring the fever down—but pills couldn't stop the rhythm of the poetry entering my body.

Mark how her turning shoulders wind the hours...
Hasten, while they are true,—sleep, death, desire...

Bind us in time, O Seasons clear, and awe.
O minstrel galleons of Carib fire,
Bequeath us to no earthly shore until
Is answered in the vortex of our grave
The seal's wide spindrift gaze toward paradise.

Vortex: 1. A whirling mass of water.
2. A whirling mass of air; especially one in the form of a visible spiral, as a tornado.
3. Something regarded as pulling into its powerful current everything that surrounds it.

Spindrift: Spray swept by a violent wind along the surface of the sea.

I couldn't understand it, but I felt it. And it felt like if I *could* understand it, or even if I came very close to understanding, I would understand the mystery of all creation.

I tried to explain it to Sandy, and she implied that maybe I had had a near-death experience and asked the doctors to keep me a few days longer. The second morning she brought me a note from Cody. It was written on a half piece of paper torn from a spiral notebook:

I guess you are pretty tough.

Cody

I smiled. I wrote a few stanzas of the poem on the back of the paper and added, *Sounds like the wind if you read it out loud.*

I gave it to Sandy to take to him. He was back at her place, with a sling around his arm. He would have to wait a while to finish the work on his car.

Everyone seemed real excited that we made it out of the twister alive. Except Dad. He was mad at me. For taking a walk. For walking with a boy. For having a secret hideout. *For being born*, I thought.

When he walked in on the second day and caught me looking up *immutable*, he got all agitated, and I figured Mom had definitely told him about me kissing Sam.

He paced back and forth between the door and the window in front of the bed. I started getting a headache turning my head back and forth to watch him. "You think you can do whatever—*feels* good." He spoke in quiet, broken sentences with long periods of silence between them. "That's not how. That's not *life*, Jesse. I would have thought. This whole mess with Missy. You are smarter. There are consequences."

After a while I finally said something back. "I don't think I can do whatever I want, Dad," I whispered. "I think maybe that's what you and Mom thought."

Dad turned toward me and his restrained voice settled on me like a giant, heavy hand. "You don't know what we were thinking," he snapped. *Neither do you*, I thought. Just then, as if a pulpit had mysteriously appeared in the hospital room, Dad's voice changed. It became eloquent, articulate—poetic, even.

"You must think about more than this moment. Wise discernment rescues the body. Guard your heart, for everything you do flows from it." Just when I was starting to get lost in his speech, thinking how good he is at speaking in meaningful tones, he pointed at the poem sitting in my lap. "Do not let yourself be turned by sinful desires and *words* that surround you."

I stared at the book and didn't dare make eye contact with

him. "I'm not like Mom," I whispered.

"No, Jesse, you're like me," he declared.

I gasped and snapped my head up.

"I don't want you to ruin your life for some good-for-nothing boy the way Missy has." His voice was tenderer.

"Why do you think Juan Pablo is good for nothing?" I waited for a response, but he didn't give one. "Because his skin is brown?"

"Of course not."

"Why is Missy's life ruined now?" I asked.

"She won't have a decent job or education. She'll be stuck in some tiny house cooking and cleaning for her kid and husband, who probably won't show up to take care of her at all."

"Oh, you mean like Mom?" I asked, pointing my finger at the small figure in the corner of the room.

Dad's face turned gray. He blinked slowly and turned around to see Mom standing there behind him. Silence as loud as that twister besieged the room. She had been in the doorway for a few minutes, waiting for a good moment to interject.

Mom looked like she just got punched in the stomach. I lowered my hand and got a sick feeling in my own stomach. I shouldn't have said that. Whatever she had done, I couldn't stand to hurt Mom on purpose like that.

Mom marched to the bed like she was hearing the very knells in her head. She moved a tray of half-eaten Jell-O and mashed potatoes to the side of the table and set down some flowers. I recognized them from the back yard. She even put some dandelions in there. Then she turned and left without looking at either one of us. It was the first time I could remember her not trying to make us feel better.

Dad turned his face back toward me looking like utter devastation. I felt sorry for him. Then I felt mad at him for making me feel sorry, so I dug in.

"Which good-for-nothing boy ruined her life, Dad?"

"That's enough!" he shouted. *Shouted.* My hands flew instinctively in front of my face like I'd been slapped. I shrunk back into the pillow. "Don't talk to me about who ruined her life." Of course. Because it was me. Me being born is what had ruined both their lives. Dad took a long breath and walked to the window then back to the bed. The machine beeped behind my head.

"I talked to Mr. Richardson today," Dad said, his calm reclaimed. "He agreed that the barn needs to be demolished."

"What?"

"The barn's coming down, Jesse."

"But—but the barn saved us—"

"You would have been better off sheltering in the ditch."

At that moment a nurse swept in through the door. "Time to change your IV!" she said cheerfully.

"I'll let you do your good work in peace," Dad said and left.

I watched the needle poke callously into my vein and winced.

"You're very brave," the nurse said, sliding her red-rimmed glasses up her nose with her knuckle.

"Not so brave," I said, remembering the look on Mom's face and thinking of Dad always getting the final say in everything.

"You're brave," the nurse repeated. "You just need to work on your timing." She glanced toward the door where Dad had just left. "There you go—all settled in for one more night."

The next day Sandy picked me up with my duffel bag and bridesmaids dress thrown in the back seat.

"Your dad said you were ready to go home," she patted my knee.

"Well, I'm not," I said.

"Maybe you should go talk to him, Sweetheart."

When I walked in the door Dad was standing at the sink, elbow deep in dirty dishes. The house was quiet as a graveyard except for the fluorescent light above his head and the muted buzzing of cicadas outside. It smelled like vinegar and lemon oil, like Mom had been trying to wash away everything that had happened in there. Wash Sam away. I almost laughed when I saw Dad; he looked so lost he may as well have been standing over the cockpit of a rocket ship. I couldn't think of a time when I'd ever seen him there before, but when I thought of Mom, I almost always pictured her in the kitchen.

"Hi," I said. It echoed off the walls.

"Welcome home. Where you should be," Dad said. He couldn't just leave it at welcome. He wiped his hands on a towel and turned toward me. "I've arranged for you to work with Mrs. Carlson at church."

"Where's Mom?" I asked. I sat down at my table that wasn't mine anymore and stared at the empty chair across from me. The chair that belonged to Sam for a short while.

"She's out." He turned back to the sink.

"*Out?* Sandy said you told her I wanted to come home, but I never said that. I want to keep staying at Sandy's. And working with her," I said. "I get paid working, you know," I added.

"You have everything you need in this house. You don't need money, and you don't need to go—with those people."

"*Those* people? You mean Sandy?" I asked him. "I'm not ready to come home and live with people who thought it was a fine idea to lie to me my whole life."

Dad turned toward me and opened his mouth, but no words came out. Behind him a cabinet door clunked an inch off its hinge. He winced. I thought of what the nurse said about timing and turned to leave.

"Where do you think you're going, young lady?"

"To pray, Dad. I'm going to pray."

12

SUNBEAMS

I didn't go pray though. Well, not exactly. I went to see Cody. I drove out to the far end of Sandy's parking lot, where Cody's car was. He had it backed up as far as he could to the edge of the vacant lot next door. That part of the parking lot was full of cheatgrass growing up through the broken asphalt. He was there, head bent over the engine, working a wrench the best he could with his left hand.

"Hey," I said.

"Hey." We stood there and looked at each other for a minute. He picked up a towel and tried to wipe the engine grease off his hand, with the same hand.

"I'm sorry about your arm," I said.

He shrugged. I went over to him, took the towel, and wiped the grease off his hand for him.

"I thought you went back to your house," he said, watching me.

"I did, but—I came back," I muttered. "I wanted to tell you thank you for saving my life."

"I didn't do that," he said shyly. "I just ran to get help. You would have survived if I wasn't there."

"No, I wouldn't have." I turned my back toward him and pulled the back of my shirt up to show the bandage next to my left shoulder blade. "If your arm wasn't there, that piece of wood would have gone through my lung," I said over my shoulder. "The nurse said it only missed it by a couple centimeters."

A warm breeze drifted across my exposed back. Cody's warm fingertips followed it and gently brushed my spine from the top down to the base. He lowered my shirt and put his hand on my hip, gently turning me toward him. His half smile creeped across his lips and he leaned down to me.

Kissing Cody made something like warm light pulse through my lips, out to my fingertips, and down to the secret part of me. He was sweet and sure. He was strong and tender. He held the back of my head like he was holding something sacred.

The next day inched by while I worked with Sandy and busied my mind with thoughts of what might happen if I found myself alone with Cody. I felt tired and dizzy each time my body tried to adjust between the heat and cold. It wasn't succeeding. I was strangely cold in the first house we visited, even though they didn't have air conditioning, but then broke into a sweat in Sandy's car with the AC blowing right on me. I managed to wash the dishes for the first two patients, but when we opened the door to the third house and flies buzzed out, I knew I was in trouble.

An elderly man shouted at us to come in—he couldn't move off the couch to open the door. Five bags of garbage greeted us, piled up just inside. My stomach reeled from the smell. Sandy looked at me with a raised eyebrow.

"Are you gonna make it in here, sweetie?" she asked.

"I'll give it a try," I said. "I need to earn my keep."

"I still think you should have stayed at home," she said. "Here, I'll haul these to the curb and maybe that will help."

She took the garbage out first thing, and I waited outside, taking a few deep breaths of the steamy air. "This is Jesse," she said on the way back in, "she's going to do the dishes, okay, handsome?"

"Oh, another angel!" the man exclaimed in a hoarse voice. "I'm surrounded by angels!"

"Did you do your exercises this week?"

"I can't move. These old bones—I couldn't move to do the exercises."

Sandy turned the TV off. I took one last breath outside and made my way through the living room, trying not to breathe. An overflowing litter box sat in the corner of the kitchen, bits of litter and cat feces spread out around it. I groaned and stepped gingerly around it.

"You have to do the exercises if you ever want to walk normally again, handsome," I heard Sandy saying from the next room.

"These old bones," the man mumbled. "Oh, you're an angel."

Sandy sneezed. I wondered just how many cats were hiding among the trash.

I poured the dish soap into the sink and tried to breathe in the lemony scent as I went to work. Luckily, this was the last house of the day. Strangely, instead of dreaming of the smell of Mom's lavender soap, I summoned the memory of Sandy's spices.

When we pulled up to Sandy's condo I looked for Cody at the far end of the parking lot. He wasn't there. My heart sank.

I walked in her door and let my eyes adjust to the darkness, the now familiar scent of incense and spices comforting me after the day. Cody was at the table reading his car magazine. His hair was wet; he must have been fresh out of the shower. This time not only was there a cat on his lap, but there was also a smaller one nestled up on the back of his neck, sleeping.

He sort of leaned his head forward so as not to disturb it. Warm light trickled through me.

"Hey," I said.

"Hey," he looked up from the magazine with his eyes while keeping his head still.

I grinned, then blushed.

Bonita looked at us, one then the other, "Hello?" she said slowly, like it was a question.

"I'll make the tea," I said, tearing my eyes from Cody. I shooed a cat off the counter.

I heard a meow and Cody suddenly appeared behind me. "I'll make it," he said. My heart beat harder. "When you make it, there's always leaves in the cup." He reached across me to pick up the teapot. Sandy scurried in the kitchen.

"Thanks, sweetie." She patted him on the back. "Jesse, will you put some food out for the cats on the front step? Thanks, sweetie."

Dinner was loud and fun and fragrant and relaxed. Sandy and Bonita bantered back and forth about the cats and the papers and the drought and the state of humanity. I laughed, and occasionally Cody smiled. With his right hand in the sling, he cut and ate the best he could with his left, which was still dirty with stubborn engine grease.

"I could help you with your car," I said out of the blue, causing Sandy and Bonita to stop ranting about politicians and the rising oceans and look at me.

"I can manage," Cody said.

"Yeah, but–it's my fault your arm is hurt. I should help you," I said.

"It's not your fault," he said.

"But I knew better," I said. "I should have gone back when I saw the clouds like that. I was just," I swallowed, "distracted." Sandy and Bonita exchanged a look. My face reddened.

"I don't want you to help me because you think you should," Cody said.

"Why don't you consider it a trade," Sandy interjected. "Jesse can be your right arm, and in exchange you can teach her about cars. Every woman ought to know how to change a tire."

"Okay," Cody shrugged.

"Okay, I'll just come round every day after work," I said as coolly as I could.

I dreamed all night about changing tires and that afternoon when I sauntered across the parking lot Cody greeted me with a tire iron in his outstretched hand, which, ironically, wasn't exactly what I had in mind when I dreamed about changing tires.

"I'll show you some stuff first," he said.

I tried to act cool and not talk too much because my mouth got dry every time he came near me. I listened without hearing as he explained the mechanics of a tire jack.

"I read that poem you gave me," he said at last, looking down at me while I sat cross-legged, attempting to loosen the bolts. "The one you said sounds like the wind."

I looked up at him. "Yeah?"

"I'm not great with poetry," he mumbled. "Give it some muscle—here—" He reached down with his good arm and pushed on the lug wrench, loosening the bolt I was struggling with. "I didn't really understand it—but, I liked the way it sounded."

"Mr. Billy says there's one word in there that took the poet nine months to pick out."

"Who's Mr. Billy?"

"He's Sandy's patient. He gave me the book."

Cody nodded. I stood up and threw all my weight on the tire iron. It loosened.

"I got it!" I shouted. He smiled. "Did you read it out loud?"

He shook his head.

"Mr. Billy says to read it out loud. I read another one he

gave me like that before, read it out loud to the prairie. It was like..." I pushed down on the next bolt, "like bringing rain to the drought."

Cody looked at me with that ember behind his eyes. He stepped forward, took the wrench out of my hand, and set it deliberately on the ground. Then he took a step closer to me and reached his left arm out to my hip. I felt the heat from his body mix with mine.

"Hey, you two!" Sandy called from halfway across the parking lot. I jumped back from him. "I've got lemonade inside. You should come in and take a break from the heat."

Cody's hand retracted, and he spun around to wave to her.

"We'll be right in!" I shouted back. I smiled awkwardly. He sighed.

For the rest of the week, the days went like that. I would work with Sandy in the morning, then go to the far end of the parking lot in the afternoons. Cody taught me how a car engine works, how to change oil and tires, what to do if it overheats. We would stay out until supper time, or until the heat drove us inside, where we would sit clumsily at Sandy's table and drink lemonade. He didn't try to kiss me again, and I worried that he only did before because of the excitement of the twister and now it had worn off.

Come Saturday my stitches were starting to itch, and my ear was starting to heal. I was restless. I asked Cody if we could take a day off from working on the car and go out to the barn. "Just to see what it's like when we're not about to die," I joked, nervous about asking him.

We walked along the dry creek bed in silence and slowed down when we got close to the barn. Slats and torn branches littered the ground around it. I smiled at my tree, bruised but still standing. Cody walked inside, watching, like the thing was going to collapse on him. The wood creaked as it warmed. Dust particles hovered in and out of the shafts of light. Cody inspected the places where the twister had blown slats off the walls and roof. He paused at the corner where we were huddled together, then kicked some hay over dried-up blood on the ground there. We looked at each other, then away. Cody shoved his hands in his pockets and dropped his head.

"Tell me about California," I said, desperate to say something so it wouldn't be obvious how badly I wanted to kiss him again.

"Um, where I live is in the forest, up north, near the coast. There are more trees than here, and it's wet and cooler. I don't think I've ever been as hot as I am here. Things grow everywhere there." He took his hands out of his pockets.

"You can always feel the ocean in the distance. Even if you can't see it or hear it, you know it's there. That's why this place feels so weird, ya know? I can't tell where the ocean is."

I nodded as if I knew what he meant. I tried to imagine what feeling the ocean would be like.

"You work on cars a lot?" I asked.

"It keeps me from doing other stuff," he shrugged. "I like it."

"How much does it cost to fix up an old car?" I asked.

"Depends on what's wrong with it and how much time you have to fix it," he said. "Why?"

"I think I need to fix up my parents' old car now that I know I'm sixteen and I can drive in other states."

"You didn't...*know*?"

I told him the whole story. Just blurted it out. "It's like I wasn't supposed to be born. I ruined things for my parents. Their futures. My life, is based on sin." It felt so good to say it out loud. It made it smaller. Like it wasn't a big deal anymore.

"I don't even understand that concept, to be honest," Cody said. "You're alive. That's it. It's done."

We sat down and I let the light coming in through the holes in the roof fall on my skin until it would get too hot, then I'd move another part of my body into the sun and let the rest of myself be in the shade.

"You know what you told me, about your car and those boys that attacked you?" I asked. "What do we—I mean, what do we do about it?"

"Nothing," he said. "It's over."

"That's not what I mean," I said. "In general, you know? I mean, what do people...like me, do about it?"

He sort of half laughed and half grunted. "Uh, build a time machine and go back and forget about ever coming to this country."

"So, how do we make it better now? Should we all leave? Go back to whatever country our ancestors came from before they immigrated here?"

He leaned down on his elbow and stretched his legs out.

"White people always think they can fix things. Or improve them—even when they don't need fixing. And then, when they can't figure out how, they just leave and move onto another place to fix. And they leave an even bigger mess. It's never about helping the people they're trying to help. It's about trying to make themselves feel better. It's them trying to numb their guilt. You can't make it better, Jesse. Look, I've seen you standing out there in the grass, I've seen you watch the sky and feel the wind and listen for thunder. You were born here. You feel the land here like I feel the ocean where I live. I can't make you go to Germany or some place."

"No one's ever noticed things like that about me," I said.

He shrugged. "Maybe the thing to do is to acknowledge it. To notice what it is and not pretend like nothing happened. Or like it doesn't matter anymore. Like *we* don't matter. Or like—we only exist in history—like we're not here now. Maybe just be thankful that you're living on our land. Most white people are either too stupid or guilty to talk about it, or they make us into bad guys so they can justify it. Some Indians are bad guys and some are good—just like white people. Nothing justifies it."

I thought about what he said. "I had a friend from school whose mother committed suicide. She shot herself in the head and didn't even care who found her," I said.

"Your friend found her?"

"Yeah. And she said the worst part was how everyone at school just ignored her like nothing had happened. She could see them looking at her funny or hear them stop talking when she came near, but no one knew what to say to her—so they said nothing. She said it wouldn't have mattered what people said. Even if they just walked up to her and said, 'I don't know what to say,' that would have been better than nothing. She just wanted people to acknowledge it. To acknowledge that her whole world had just changed."

Cody nodded. "Maybe that's what I mean. I don't really know. Most of the time I try not to think about it." He picked up a stick and started making lines in the dirt. He looked up shyly. "When I first got here, and you asked me about that stupid bumper sticker—you were acknowledging something. Like, I'm an Indian and you're white, and we don't walk through this world in the same way. People walk around like they know, but they don't. No one bothers to ask. But you did. Even fewer people bother to listen. Maybe you don't understand—but you listen, and that's something."

"It doesn't feel like enough."

"Can anything ever be enough?" He threw his unhurt arm behind his head and laid back. "What about you?" he asked. "Are you going to confront your parents? Or stay at Sandy's until you graduate?"

"I don't want to go back home," I said. "It's easier if I don't talk to them. I can never come up with words when I talk to my dad. I never say the right thing. Or think the right thing or do the right thing."

"The right thing for who?" he asked quietly, looking at me for a second, then returning his eyes to the sky.

"I don't know." I picked up his stick. "I can't even make tea right," I mumbled.

"What?"

"The other day—you made the tea because I leave too many leaves in the pot."

Cody leaned up on his elbow and half smiled in the way I was beginning to know well.

"I made the tea because I wanted to be near you," he said. My skin tingled. "Forget about humanity and racism and your parents and whether or not you were supposed to be born for a minute. You're alive now. What do you want to do right now, Jesse? For you?"

There was only one answer to that question and thinking about it made me lose my breath. I brought my mouth to his, hoping to get my breath from him. We didn't say anything else. We melted into the thick, humid air. The sun between the slats played all over my body, and I couldn't tell what was Cody's hand and what was the light—they were both so warm and soft. We transfigured into fractals of light, glistening across the walls of the barn, making it impossible to tell the difference between us and the sunbeams. Particles of dust, or maybe they were stars, danced inside us. We were as buoyant as sunlight. As bright and warm and transparent as the light.

13

THE DEVIL INSIDE

By the time Sandy and I headed out to Mr. Billy's place again, I still hadn't figured it out.

"Maybe he'll give me a hint," I said.

"About what?" Sandy asked, turning the music down to hear me better. I had insisted on listening to the same mix CD she made me on the first day until I had all the songs memorized.

"The nine-month word in this poem."

"Oh, yes, he might have a hint—but he'll probably make you work for it. That's what he did to me when I was his student."

"What do you mean? You were his student?"

"Didn't I tell you? Mr. Billy was the head of the English department at Wichita State when I went to school there. You know—after the van broke down—after the Keeper of the Plains—I went back to school finally."

"I guess I assumed you went to nursing school."

"I did, eventually. But first I finished my undergrad degree at Wichita State."

"How did a college professor end up all alone out here?

With no one to look after him?"

"Anyone can end up alone," Sandy warned. "He has kids, but they don't approve of him. Don't accept him for who he is. I think he made a choice to live honestly a long time ago, even if it meant being alone. Besides, we're not no one. We're looking after him."

We pulled up to his mobile and the forest around his home looked thinner. Some of the trees had lost their leaves; others were just smaller versions of their normal summer selves. The drought was beginning to kill indiscriminately. We entered Mr. Billy's home, and there he sat—in the same position. I smiled.

"Hello, handsome," Sandy hollered and kissed him on the top of his head. The room was humid and stuffy. Mr. Billy didn't waste time on hellos.

"Well, little darling?" he asked, looking at me.

I sighed and slumped down on the window seat in between a stack of books and a cactus. "I need help," I said. "I don't get it."

"Get what?"

"The poem."

"You mean, you don't understand it," he said.

"Right. I looked up all the words—and I understand their meaning, but—put together? I just don't know."

"Hmph."

"I read it out loud."

"Good."

"I read it outside."

"What *do* you get?" he asked.

"Well, it seems like—obviously there's the part about the ocean."

"What about her?"

"Um, that her shoulders wind the hours?" Mr. Billy was silent. "That you could drown. But it's also beautiful. There's a boat, I think. And the Caribbean...music?"

"Listen, little darlin'," he fixed his one eye on me. "You're namin' the parts. But you didn't listen to the whole. Think." He leaned back and coughed.

I opened the book to the poem and read through it again silently. The sound of clinking dishes and running water drifted over from the kitchen. Mr. Billy's breathing was heavy. I got to the end and looked up at him.

"Love?"

He smiled.

"You're getting there." He leaned in toward me. "Keep looking for that word."

"Okay, I will."

Sandy and I headed out into the wall of heat and told Mr. Billy we'd be back next week. We started toward Zeus's house, and this time I was armed not only with a spade to pull the dandelions but also a bottle of bleach and plastic gloves in case we encountered any more cat litter situations after that. I can learn. The music was fast and loud and made me feel like dancing, not that I'd ever tried it. It made me feel invincible. It went straight to my heart and strengthened it, made it beat with fire. We hadn't been on the road for too long when Sandy got a call from her office.

There was some kind of emergency at a patient's house. Sandy looked over at me with a worried expression.

"I've got Jesse with me today," she said into the phone. "Isn't there someone else who can go?" She sighed, turned her blinker on, and pulled off onto a side road.

"Okay, sweetie," she said. "We've gotta go check up on Kim. Apparently, her father called the office because she called him in hysterics. You remember her and Floyd? It doesn't sound good."

"What's going on? Should we call the police?" I asked.

"They called the police already. They're on their way, but

you know how far we are from the station. Don't worry, this is what I do. I can handle it. I'll just go in first to see if I can calm everybody down. Here's what we're gonna do: You stay in the car, okay, sweetie? If something seems...wrong, you just keep my phone and call your dad to come pick you up."

"What?"

"Can you do that, Jesse?"

"Why would I do that?"

"Just stay in the car, okay?"

The car bounced over the potholes, and Sandy didn't seem to care about slowing down or driving around them. We reached the mobile home, which was standing in the direct sun with no shade. *It must be like an oven in there*, I thought. Sandy grabbed her purse from the back seat and walked up to the door without another word. I rolled the windows down so I wouldn't bake and looked down at the phone. I heard muffled shouting from inside and couldn't tell if it was Floyd and Kim or the TV. The sun reflected off the white walls and stung my eyes. I heard music from the TV and felt relieved–it wasn't them shouting. Then a shriek sounded through the thin walls so real I jumped.

I got out of the car and ran toward the house. I stood at the threshold, listening. Suddenly Sandy burst through the door looking behind her like she expected a bear to come out.

"C'mon Kim!" she yelled. I stumbled back toward the car.

Crashing sounds came from inside, glass breaking. A pregnant woman came to the door. She had a dirty face, and haggard clothes and looked–just sad. Her feet were swollen, her hair hung down around her eyes.

"I can't," she whimpered to Sandy. "I can't." She started to silently cry. Tears poured down and left tracks on her dirty cheeks. She didn't wipe them.

"Yes, you can," Sandy whispered back, emphasizing each word. "Now get in the car. Now."

Then I heard a holler come from inside that sent shivers through me.

"Kim!" It roared. "Kim, where the hell you think you're going?" Floyd came to the door. I could smell him from back by the car. He was even dirtier than before, and his cheeks were sunken in. He had a wet spot down the front of his trousers, like he'd peed himself. The lower part of his right leg was covered in wet blood that ran down onto his bare foot. The woman shrunk down and turned away.

"You think you're leaving me?" he screeched, then changed his expression and softened. He stepped down on the first cinder-block step and crushed a cicada under his bare foot. I winced. He didn't notice. "You can't leave me," he whimpered. "I need you, baby. I need you." He swayed and put his hand up to the door frame for support.

"You think you can just go whenever you want? Well? Answer me, woman!" Floyd screamed, working his way back to angry. Kim didn't answer, so he grabbed her by her hair and pulled her head up to his face and shouted even louder, right in her ear. "I asked you a question! I asked you where the hell you think you're going, woman!" Floyd emphasized every other word by pushing his face closer to Kim's, then rearing back for the next one. Then he lost his balance altogether and fell forward, down the cinder-block steps, but he didn't let go of Kim's hair, and she was pulled down on top of him. "Get offa me!" He pushed her away, and she rolled up in a little ball in the dirt.

"That's enough, Floyd!" Sandy shouted.

"You." He pushed himself up and turned toward Sandy. "You got no right coming here! This is *your* fault!" He tripped and fell as best he could toward Sandy, any tenderness that had been there, gone. Out of the corner of his eye he noticed me. "Who's that?" he sneered, pointing.

Sandy's shoulders dropped, and her breath got heavy. She

didn't take her eyes off him. "No one," she said. "You're seeing things."

"The hell I am!" He turned and barreled down the drive toward me. I froze. Next thing I knew, he had me by the hair. I raised my arms, clawed at his tangled fingers. He pulled me toward Sandy. "If she ain't real, how come I can touch her?" Mangled messes of arms wriggled against my face, my hands prying them off, pain like a hot iron burning my scalp. I couldn't think, I could only feel. Pain. Fear. I tried to run. He shook me. Sandy shouted.

I heard a gunshot.

He released his grip on my hair, and we both looked up to see Sandy standing in front of us, pointing a gun at him.

"I said let her go," Sandy demanded. Her shirt shook with fear, but her hands were steady. "Get in the car, Jesse, and turn it on."

I stumbled toward the car, but I saw the pregnant lady balled up next to the door. After feeling what it was like to get your hair pulled like that, I couldn't leave her there in the dirt to keep feeling it. I snuck over to her, pulled at her arms until she sat up, then tried to push her toward the car.

We didn't make it. Floyd started hollering, saying I was kidnapping his girlfriend. He grabbed her like she was a sack of potatoes and carried her back up toward the mobile.

"You're not leaving here woman! You can't leave me! I need you. I need you." He started to cry, his body racked with sobs, then he lifted his fists to the sky and brought them down onto Kim's back. "Why you make me need you so bad?" he sobbed as he hit her.

I grabbed his arm. He looked at me, and I swear the Devil himself was in those eyes. He shook me away and slammed his fist directly into my injured ear. Warm blood trickled down my neck. I brought my hand up to my ear and fell down, crunching into the gravel with my bare elbows and knees.

Sirens rang in my head and my eyes went black. Sandy shouted something inaudible. Pain shot through my knees and elbows and stole my breath.

But it was almost a good feeling—because I recognized it.

I'd skinned my knees a hundred times as a kid. I knew what this pain meant. I knew there'd be bits of stone stuck in my skin and blood and dirt mixing together. I knew Mom would have to clean it out with peroxide. I laid my cheek down in the gravel and smelled the dirt.

Floyd kicked me clumsily, tried to lift Kim. The muscles in my calves pulsated with blood where he'd kicked them. I knew then, for certain, that they were there. So I stood on them, felt them some more.

Sandy fired another shot.

She looked in a daze. Floyd had abandoned Kim and was shouting something fierce, kicking up dust and throwing his hands all around, like he was fighting some phantom only he could see. Sandy stood there, holding the gun at him with a look in her eye that made me tremble.

The look a person gets when they've decided to kill somebody.

No one was coming. I knew that. The cops weren't there. Dad wasn't there. Jesus wasn't there. And Sandy—something in her eyes wasn't there either. It was up to me. A strange thought came to me. I remembered what Sandy had told me the very first time I went for a ride with her: Things only have the power we decide to give them. I decided I wasn't going to give power to that man.

"*Fear not for I am with you,*" I said out loud to myself. I stumbled for a minute, trying not to black out, then made my way over to Sandy and stood between her and Floyd.

"Put the gun down, Sandy," I said. She didn't budge. "You don't want to kill nobody, Sandy," I said. "It would change you."

"Get out of the way, Jesse. I'm not letting this happen again. I'm not letting him hurt us anymore—I'm in charge this time—I'm not letting him hurt her ever again." Her normally sparkling eyes were like coal.

"Put the gun down, Sandy!" I shouted.

She startled, like she was coming out of a trance. Floyd stopped throwing punches at the air and looked at us, pale and wobbly, like he might collapse.

"That's not your mom, Sandy," I whispered.

She blinked, then sucked in several short breaths, her chest heaving. She leaned down on her knees, her face screwed up in pain, and started hyperventilating.

It was quiet for a second.

Floyd snorted, grabbed Kim's arm, and pulled her to the steps. She let out a long, sad, beaten wail and let herself be pulled along.

"Stop!" I demanded. "Leave her be."

Floyd laughed until he coughed. "What are you gonna do about it?" he sneered, revealing black teeth.

I had no idea what I was going to do about it. "*God, my rock and my shelter*," I said the only thing I could think of, "*He delivered me from my strong enemy.*"

Floyd let out a long, high-pitched laugh, like it was the funniest thing he'd ever heard.

"Oh, you must be a comedian or something! Do you think God is real? Grow up little girl!" he shouted. Then drawled, "There's no God. There's only *men*."

"I didn't say it for you. It's for her," I said, nodding at Kim.

Floyd let go of her arm and tried to focus his shifting eyes on me. She dropped in a heap at his feet and he tripped over her legs on his way toward me. The ringing in my head got louder. So loud even Floyd heard it and looked behind me. I turned and saw Bobby Lindbergh Junior racing up the drive in his truck, siren wailing. Floyd immediately lifted his palms above his head like he hadn't done a thing.

Sandy rushed to Kim and began taking her vitals. The top of my head started to tingle, and a wave of cold chills poured down from my head, through my insides, and down to my toes.

Bobby jumped out of the truck, telling someone on the radio to send an ambulance. "Jesse, what are you doing here? You okay?"

It felt like the inside of my body was completely empty. I couldn't breathe because I didn't have lungs. I sunk to my knees and threw up on Bobby's shoes.

14

FRENCH SILK CHOCOLATE PIE

For the second time that summer my parents met me at the hospital. This time I was conscious, though. I had a few scrapes and bruises, but the real damage was my ear. The doctors said I would never hear out of it again. I figured that meant I was half-deaf, and I was pretty sure half-deaf people didn't get to college on singing scholarships.

I tried real hard to still be mad at Mom and Dad, but when they walked in the door, faces smeared with tears and worry, suddenly I needed them.

I heard pieces of Dad's admonishment of Sandy in the hallway outside my room.

"How *dare* you...my daughter in danger...a *gun*...we trusted you...let us down."

Sandy's sobs drowned out half of what he said.

Mom sat next to the bed, holding my hand and praying—but it wasn't peaceful. She mumbled to herself and stopped to cry halfway through.

"This is my fault. I'm being punished for my sins. I drove you away and look what's happening. This is all my fault."

Nothing seemed to matter anymore. Not Mom and Sam,

not their lies. I slept that night squished in bed between Mom and Dad, like I did when I was little and had a nightmare. I wanted to disappear inside their hugs and never return to the world again. I wanted to be protected. But no amount of hugging and reassuring can protect you from what's inside. Just like when I was little, when morning came and I survived, I knew I had to face the next night on my own.

I spent the day trying to be normal, trying to do all the things I did before, but that went too far back. Before Sam, before rock music, before Mom's lie, before Cody's story. I was too changed—I didn't feel like me anymore.

I helped Mom clean the house and made sun tea and read for a while. I used Mom's method and tried to clean the memory of Floyd out of my brain by scouring the bathtub and the sink and scrubbing the floors. His twisted mouth with bits of spit forming in the corners as he shouted at me—out. His fist, red knuckles and white nails caked with dirt—out with the smell of bleach sucking in through my nose. His bloodshot eyes, so mean—out with the steel wool. Scrub it out.

But when I tried to clean the blood off the shirt I was wearing the day before, I realized I was running the whole thing through my head over and over again.

Mom walked in on me crying at the bathroom sink, which was full of blood. My hands were so raw from the bleach and scrubbing they were starting to bleed at the knuckles. She decided we had to face it straight on. And that mean: pie.

Mom sat us down at the table in front of a large French silk chocolate pie, her best pie of all, still believing in the everlasting healing power of eating. I stared at it.

"The thing is," I said slowly, "part of me wanted her to kill him. He was awful—I thought, *it would be better for everyone if he was dead.*" I began to sob inwardly; tears didn't come, but my body shook.

Mom took a huge bite of pie and furrowed her brow.

"How does that make me any different than him?" I asked.

Her fork scraped the cream from the plate.

"Because you didn't," she said. "You didn't let her kill him." She helped herself to more pie. "You might not be so different from that man and him from you—except that you have your eyes open, looking for the good in things. Looking for the good in yourself. *Your eye is the lamp of your body. If your eye is healthy, your whole body is full of light,* that's what Jesus said. That man's eyes are closed to goodness—even though there's goodness in him."

"*Therefore consider whether the light in you is not darkness*," I quoted. "What about the evil in me? How does God decide who suffers and who doesn't? Why was that poor lady made to be beaten by that horrible man? How could that happen ten miles away while I'm here eating pie?"

"Because you were lucky enough to be born into different circumstances than her."

"But why? Why was I lucky and she wasn't?" I asked.

"It is not our job to understand," Mom said. "What does God ask of us, Jesse? He does not ask that we suffer when we see others' suffering; just that we love."

"This is too much," I whispered, tears coming at last. "This is too hard."

"It is hard," she sighed. "Life is hard. Otherwise, we'll never be ready to die."

"Jeez, Mom!"

"Don't swear, Jesse."

"Why not?!"

"Just—here, just eat some pie. It'll make you feel better."

Pie, not surprisingly, did make me feel better. Better enough to feel pressed upon by the sterility of my house, as if the air itself had sharp edges. Better enough to feel suffocated by the heaviness of the silence there. Better enough to know I didn't quite belong there, at my table, and to wish I was sitting at Sandy's instead. Mom wrapped up the remaining pie and wiped off the table.

"Missy's baby's home from the hospital, did you hear?" Mom asked. "According to her mom she's just the sweetest thing in the world. So sweet it made her forget how mad she was, I guess."

"Maybe I'll go see her," I said.

"I'll bet she'd appreciate that, honey. Here—why don't you take her this extra pie."

I drove into town, but before I went to Missy's, I just had to go to Sandy. She opened the door and a deluge of apologies rained over me. "I can't begin to tell you how sorry I am for putting you in that situation. I should have never gone there with you. I should have never had the gun—I'm so sorry, Jesse." Her words ran out of her mouth like she had a motor in there on overdrive. I couldn't keep them straight. She began to weep in her hands. "You saved my life," she sobbed. "You saved my life."

Bonita came to the door and reached her hand up to Sandy's. She ushered her toward the table. "Thank you," Bonita said to me. "Thank you. Sit. I'll make the tea for once."

Just then Cody burst through the door out of breath. He stopped short when he saw me.

"I saw your car pull up," he said. "You're okay?"

"I guess. I'm deaf in this ear," I said, pointing to my left ear.

"Sit," Bonita called from the kitchen.

We all sat around the table and drank tea in silence. That table that had given me such comfort and warmth when I needed it—now it was changed, too. The condo was clean and tidy, dark and quiet—no music came from the record player. No food was cooking. The spices and incense smelled stale, and strange. I had no place anymore. I stared at the bottom of my empty cup.

"I just want to understand," I broke the silence at last, "why that lady—Kim—was there with that man. Why didn't she leave a long time ago? Why was he so horrible?"

"Those are questions without answers," Bonita said. "We don't know what Floyd was like before he became an addict. We don't know what passes between two people. Look at us around this table—we've all experienced suffering and injustice."

"Not me," I breathed. "Not like that." I looked at them. "Not like you."

"Look at the grass growing on the prairie—even through the drought," Bonita continued. "Look at the weeds that choke out the flowers, and yet they feed the butterflies. Look at the mouse eating the grasshopper and the hawk eating the mouse, they die—though we know—life wants to live. Look at how you helped my Sandy in a moment of confusion and fear. Jesse, the cosmos is infinitely complex. We must endeavor to raise our wakefulness to the point where we surpass the need for an explanation."

Cody reached out and held my hand. His arm was out of the sling, and stitches etched a crooked line across his skin like a railroad track. I closed my eyes and I swear I felt light pouring from his hand into my body.

"Choose beauty," Bonita said. "Then give *everything* you've got to preserve it. To help it grow."

Cody walked me to my car. "I need to go home," I told him. "I'm sorry. I just—I don't belong here." He kissed me. That felt different, too. But not foreign or suffocating, it felt like harborage in a storm.

Missy, thankfully, was still Missy.

"Oh my God, Jesse, you look terrible! You look worse than me, and I'm the one who just had a baby—I'm just kidding! C'mon—wash your hands and come see little Maria. Can you believe how big my boobs are? Oh my God, they're humongous."

That's not really a word, I thought.

"I had to name her Maria because otherwise JP's mom would have totally freaked out. Oh my God, Jesse, I'm so tired. You have no idea how tired I am. Can you watch her right now so I can go take a nap? I'm just kidding. But, seriously, the sleepiness is out of control. Do you want to change her diaper? We named her middle name Stephanie, which is what I wanted, so you can call her Stephanie if you want to."

I watched Missy unhook her bra and shove a gigantic nipple into little Maria Stephanie's mouth. I don't mean *very big,* I mean *gigantic*. Amazingly, the child took it and suckled.

"Whoa, Mis, your boobs *are* seriously big," I said.

"I know, right? What happened to your ear?" she asked.

"Oh, it's kind of a long story—but I got caught out in that twister and a nail went through it. I can't hear out of it anymore."

"Jesse! What were you doing out in the storm?"

"Just being super lucky I didn't die, I guess. How are you, Missy? How is everything going?"

"It's so hard. I'm not gonna lie; It's *so* hard. I thought I was dying the other night because I was so tired. She throws up like, all the time all over me—they call it spit up, but it is just straight-up barf. I'm lucky, though, because JP's mom and his aunt help me every day. My mom, too, sometimes. She comes over—she asked me to move back in with her and Daddy—can you believe that?"

Missy looked down at her baby, and tears filled her eyes.

"You know, Jesse, people kept saying how me and JP was in trouble, remember? When I got pregnant they kept saying how he *got* me in trouble. Well, she's a lot of trouble, there's no doubt about that," she laughed, "but, we made a human. It's not like when you stay out past curfew and you get in trouble—it's a little person who depends on you. I have to be better now, ya know? I have to think about someone other than myself."

I held Maria Stephanie after she was done drinking. She was still impossibly small but much bigger than when I saw her at the hospital.

"You know what the doctor told me?" Missy asked, watching Maria Stephanie wiggle in my arms while she stuffed a towel in her bra. "She said human babies are the most helpless of all the creatures on Earth."

I looked down and shook my head. "How do we ever survive?" I asked. Maria Stephanie started to cry.

"Love," Missy said, lifting the baby from my arms. "Just 'cause our parents love us so much."

"You're gonna be a good mom, Missy," I said.

"What do you mean, *gonna* be?" she asked. "I'm good now! Just kidding. But you gotta go now, Jesse, 'cause it's nap time, and I seriously need to sleep."

15

PRAIRIE FIRE

Light poured in through the sanctuary windows. Mrs. Carlson had removed the sheets that hung over them to block out the sun.

"I know it will get hot later, but we need to see, for Pete's sake!" she said. "If we work early enough, we'll be done for the day before the heat settles in."

I sat in the middle pew, five rows back, and watched the morning light stream in. Dust particles wove in and out of the sunbeams. The wooden pew creaked underneath me, warming up. The earthy smell of wood mixed with brewing coffee. After being away so long, the sanctuary appeared small to me. It wrapped itself around me—the embrace of my parents. It was a comfort so deep and so specific to this tiny place that my heart ached, knowing somehow it was slipping away from me.

Dad had come home the night before with a speech prepared about how I wasn't allowed to ever see Sandy, or any of her relations, again. There would be no more reading of poetry, and I had to be inside the house before dark. My car privileges were taken away; I was only allowed to drive to church and back. He only noticed I was curled up with the

Bible on the couch listening to Chopin after he'd finished. I just stared at him. He cleared his throat, "Well." That was it.

My job that morning was to collect all the hymnals and song books from the pews and go through them, page by page, to make sure they weren't drawn in, colored on, torn out, or otherwise defaced.

"I would prefer to order new ones," Mrs. Carlson said, peering over her reading glasses. "These are as old as me! But your daddy says if we have some already—"

"Waste not, want not," I recited.

"Well, you know how it goes, dear," she said. "We best hurry—the heat's coming in fast this morning. I think in about an hour we'll have to close up the windows and break for the day."

We sat together, flipping through pages, Mrs. Carlson chatting away.

"Deary me, just look at this, Jesse. Can you believe some people let their children ruin books like this?" she pointed at a page with crayon scribbled over it.

"They probably didn't notice the kid was doing it," I mumbled. "Parents don't notice a lot of things."

"Oh my, look at this! What sort of deviant wrote this?" She looked up in delicious shock and reveled in showing me a swear word neatly printed in the corner of one of the pages. "Teenagers," she said shortly, like I wasn't one. She pulled out an eraser and scrubbed the page clean. "This drought has all but killed every one of my rose bushes," she sighed. "Completely brown! Then come the grasshoppers, you know. I'm trying to pray, Jesse, like your daddy says. I'm really praying hard, but we don't seem to have a drop of rain."

"I'm not really convinced it works like that," I mumbled, erasing pencil lines that someone had drawn, underlining every time the word *Jesus* appeared in the text.

"Our pear trees have gone completely dormant, thanks be

to God, as if it's the dead of winter. But at least they haven't died altogether. Of course some won't come back, you know. Some will never come back."

"Some will come back stronger," Dad said, walking in with a cup of coffee. "Time to close the curtains ladies." He smiled. I glared. "Jesse, you go on home now, okay?"

"Okay," I said.

"Just home."

"I said okay."

That evening I sat at the kitchen table and watched Mom take a casserole out of the oven. Dad was bent in a crooked, unnatural way holding a screwdriver, which, in his hands looked like a cave man holding a cell phone, trying to fix the broken cabinet door. They were pretending. I had played house enough with Missy to recognize the game when I saw it.

Dad dropped the screwdriver yet again and slammed his fist down hard on the counter.

"Jesse, how about if you go put on some music?" he said.

I walked to the living room and stood in front of the record player, staring at the records on the shelf.

"What if—we started listening to some different kinds of music?" I asked toward the kitchen.

"The music we have is fine," Dad droned.

"It's the most beautiful music in the world," Mom agreed.

"How do you know?" I asked, moving to the entryway of the kitchen and leaning on the doorframe. "What if there is some other real great music out there and we don't know it because we only listen to classical?"

"Jesse, when is this going to stop?" Dad complained. "When am I going to get my little girl back?"

"I'm not little anymore, Dad."

"You'll always be our little girl, Jesse—that's what he meant," Mom chimed in.

"I met the Devil this summer—and it ain't music," I said.

"It's *not* music—"

"Thank you, Mom."

"I didn't mean—"

"Our music is fine, and that's final."

He could say it, but nothing felt final anymore.

"Claude Debussy was the rock star of his time. I'm just saying."

I met Cody out at the barn the next day after helping Mrs. Carlson with the hymnals. I tried to convince myself it wasn't lying if I just didn't mention it, but somewhere inside I knew I was being like them, and I hated it. Cody told me about cars, ocean currents, and temperate rain forests. I told him about classical music, cicadas, and virga.

"How can it rain but not rain?" he asked.

"It rains in the sky, from the clouds, but the air is so dry and hot that it evaporates before it hits the ground."

"That's weird."

We read Mr. Billy's books, which I had stashed out there, and tried to figure out what they meant. And we kissed. I told him about the monarchs. He told me about how he almost drowned once, right near the shore in a storm current. He had tried to stand up, but the undertow was too strong; it pulled his feet out from under him, then the waves came from behind and pushed his face into the sand, over and over again. It was Sandy who finally ran into the dragging tide to tear him out of its grip.

"I couldn't hold my breath anymore—I was starting to take in water," he said. "One more second—The ocean is...I can't even describe the power."

He stroked my hair. I ran my fingers along the crooked scar on his forearm. I asked after Sandy and Bonita. He said they had taken in another cat. *To replace me,* I joked. We left in order for us both to be home in time for dinner, me walking down the dry creek bed, Cody striding across the plain to where his car was parked up on the ridge.

The next day at church I finished looking through the hymnals for curse words and scribbles, so Dad invented another job categorizing all the songs—songs about love, songs about faith, songs about fear.

A strange sort of peacefulness settled into me that hadn't been there since before the summer. The weather noticed it too. It still didn't rain, but the air became a bit cooler. It was still hot enough to keep the curtains closed all day, but instead of a wall of heat, it was a door. The drought granted us a passageway out into the land—one that didn't leave us feeling beat up. The grass had turned all shades of brown and yellow, and only the strongest, or greediest, trees still had green on their branches.

"You'll never believe what happened, Jesse!" Mrs. Carlson said swooping into the sanctuary. "My pear trees are blooming—like it's spring! It's a miracle," she became reverent. "Blossoms in summer, and here I thought they would die. Oh, ye of little faith, eh, Jesse?"

"The Lord works in mysterious ways," I told her what she wanted to hear.

"Praise God from Whom all blessings flow." She began flipping through a hymnal. "Did you hear about Bobby Junior? Asked your dad this morning if he could book the church for his wedding! Good, God-fearing boy—that Morgan caught a good one. I guess John Richardson hired him to tear down some old barn on his property—gonna start work in a couple days. He said he and Morgan will come by when he's done and talk to us about what music they'd like at the wedding. I don't know, Jesse, maybe you should categorize these based on tempo and vocal range instead of content. What do you think?"

I blinked back the tears burning my eyes. "I think Dad is making up work to keep me out of trouble," I said honestly.

"Oh, Jesse, you're funny. Just make a note for me, if you don't mind, of the tempo, okay? You know most of these, don't you? Of course you do. You'll have my job before too long!" With that she flitted off to the fellowship hall.

I focused on the hymns to distract me from the aching in my heart. I started writing down song numbers in long columns. Then I dared to hum the ones I knew, which it turned out were a lot.

I was alone in the sanctuary. *Why do these have to be so long*, I wondered. I laid down in the pew like I used to when I was a kid—lying there coloring or daydreaming, hard, cool wood pressing against my cheek, the sound of Dad's voice lulling me to sleep. I came across Mom's favorite hymn: "Be Thou My Vision." We sung it every Easter. But she hummed it to herself sometimes around the house, dusting, mopping, vacuuming. A pang of guilt pulsed through my heart. *She's always cleaning*, I thought.

I hummed the first few lines, and the sanctuary echoed the notes back to me. I heard it in my good ear. I sat up and sang it out a bit louder, following the notes closely along the page. It was the first time I had dared to sing since hurting my ear. I was scared I couldn't do it anymore, that my hearing would be different. But it felt the same as before. It felt sort of like reading Mr. Billy's book to the prairie. I stood up and sang it out as loud and strong as I could. The walls vibrated. Dust particles swirled. My perfectly unimpaled heart pumped, my lungs filled with breath, my diaphragm lowered, sound escaped from my body, and then—my body disappeared.

The sound was free.

I raised my arms and tossed my head back, letting the hymnal fall with a thump to the bench. After all, I knew this one by heart. My body tingled with a sensation that only comes from completely losing yourself, allowing your body to drift away and, at the same time, letting something flow through it.

For a few seconds at the end of the song the room echoed, then everything became still again. The dust settled; the wood creaked. The room looked the same. But the silence had been changed.

"You sure do have a pretty singing voice, Jesse. Clear as a bell." Mrs. Carlson thumped down another pile of books. Dust rose from them.

I sat down and reluctantly started categorizing again. *It's impossible to separate the ones about love from the ones about faith or fear,* I thought. None of them were one or the other. I came up on one I didn't know: Psalm 107. It was your typical psalm, talking about God saving us from our enemies with His steadfast love, His power being almighty and all that, but then, one line caught my eye:

> *"For He commanded and raised the stormy wind,*
> *which lifted up the waves of the sea."*

Goosebumps trickled down my arms and legs. I dropped the hymnal onto the pew and the thump rang out through the sanctuary. I stood up.

"*Bind us in time, O Seasons clear,*" I said out loud. I ran out of the church. I didn't care what Dad would say, I hopped in the Brown Bomber and headed out to see Mr. Billy.

I drove up Mr. Billy's long driveway and stared out at the familiar shadows the cottonwoods threw across the dirt road. The sun felt warm instead of scorching. The leaves on the trees were mostly brown and sparse, making the forest seem empty and lonely.

I ran through my head what I was going to say to Mr. Billy when I got there. I would walk straight up to him, glint in my eye, and lean over that statue in an easy chair and look right in his good eye and say just one word. The nine-month word.

I smiled as I thought about it. But when I surged through his front door triumphantly, he wasn't there. My whole body sagged, and I let out a deep sigh.

"Mr. Billy! Mr. Billy, it's Jesse," I called out. There was no answer. I waited a few moments in case he was in the bathroom. I ran my hand across his books—there was a new stack sitting by his chair. "Mr. Billy!" I shouted again. Nothing. Finally, I peeked around the corner of the kitchen. The dishes were stacked neatly in the sink, waiting for Sandy to come clean them. He wasn't there.

I went outside and let the smell of the forest come over me. I stood there and looked around at what Mr. Billy looked at every day. A chickadee chirped from a high branch. A Nuthatch hopped headfirst down the deep ravines of the cottonwood. I spied a cicada shell stuck to the bark and smiled as I plucked it off and set it on the stoop for Mr. Billy to find.

Then I noticed something bright red in the distance, a bit beyond the row of cottonwoods behind his house. I stumbled onto a little, worn-out track in the dirt. It looked like Mr. Billy walked this way all the time. I guess he wasn't just sitting in that chair all day long after all. I guess he was out there looking for snake skins and turtle shells. There was a meadow behind the row of trees, with grass and a few boulders. And there was a small patch of land covered with Prairie Fire crabapple trees. And they were in bloom. Bright red flowers reflected the sun and made the forest look like it was lit with the fire of the sun. It was the most beautiful thing I'd ever seen, just like Mr. Billy said.

Then I saw him. Crumpled up next to a big boulder, looking like a heap of old, brown leaves waiting to be burned. I ran to him.

"Mr. Billy!"

He moaned. I kneeled down and rolled him over. He was dying. I don't know how I knew, but I knew if I left to go call the ambulance he'd be dead before I got back. So I put his head on my lap. He smelled like mildew. He struggled to open his eyes. His breath was wheezy and short. I looked around, desperately wishing someone else would be there.

"Prairie Fire crabapples," I said. "They're so beautiful." He wheezed and coughed weakly. I took a deep breath and thought, *What would I want to hear if I was lying here dying*? He closed his eyes. I swallowed hard.

"I want you to know how much I love those books you gave me. I want to say thank you for them." I put my hand on his forehead and rubbed my thumb along the deep lines there. "I want you to know I think you're a really good man," I said, "and that I'm really going to miss you." His breaths became farther and farther apart. "Hey, Mr. Billy," I whispered. I leaned in real close to his ear so he would hear me: "*Spindrift*."

He opened his mouth like he was trying to take a breath, but no air went in. Then he let out one last breath and went totally still. At that moment, a gust of wind blew in through the meadow and blood-red blossoms rained down all around us. They floated through the air and twirled with the gust, then settled on the ground, turning the grass to fire. The trees whistled and rattled a sweet and mournful song. Then as quickly as it came, the wind was gone.

I don't know how long I sat there. I felt like a glassy lake. I didn't move my hand from Mr. Billy's forehead. Everything around me was exactly the same as it was the moment before he died. I tried to comprehend that. The crabapple blossoms stirred in the breeze. The cottonwoods creaked and moaned like they always did. The chickadee chirped. The sun moved slowly along the sky and heated my back. Little ants crawled around the boulder.

Finally, I had to move because my legs were numb. I laid down on the Prairie Fire and stretched them out, waiting for the feeling to return.

Okay, I thought as the hot needle pain in my legs started pricking me, *I'm alive*.

16

I'M ALIVE

I closed my eyes, and images washed over them; memories of the summer seeped through my pores. Cody's arm twisting a wrench. Mr. Billy, cold and pale on the ground. The funnel cloud. Lightning. Sam's salty-sweet breath. Red trees. The train whistle. Cody's lips on my neck. Kim, beat-up and crying. Sandy's gun. Lake swimming. The ringing in my ear. Mom's face, full of shame. The wind on the tall grass. Blood running down my shirt. Cody's dark eyes.

Far away, I heard the sound of cars and trucks pulling into the drive and Sandy calling Mr. Billy's name. My head cleared, like a wave crashed through my brain and pulled the images back out to sea. I sat up.

"Over here!" I shouted.

Two EMTs, Sandy, and Cody ran over to me. Sandy fell on the ground next to Mr. Billy and began to weep. I shook my head at the EMTs. Cody looked at Mr. Billy and his brow furrowed; he turned around and took a few steps away. I scooped up a handful of fire blossoms and put them in my pocket.

"Hey," I said, walking to Cody.

"You okay?" he asked.

My lip quivered. He hugged me and rubbed my back as I cried into his chest.

"How'd you know to come?" I asked.

"He called her," Cody said. "Said he didn't feel well."

Sandy sat over Mr. Billy, her eyes closed, chanting in a language I'd never heard. The EMTs went to the edge of the meadow, sat on a rock, and waited patiently.

"Will you go out to the barn with me tonight?" I asked Cody.

"Of course."

"Will you spend the night out there with me?" I asked.

He froze and stared back at me. His breath quickened. "Okay."

Mom was busy cooking up my favorite casserole when I got home. She looked up at me and sighed when I walked in.

"You've had a heck of a summer, kid," she said.

"Mom, you just swore."

She looked at me straight on. "Forgive me," she said.

I tilted my head and looked at her with a question in my eyes. "Sandy called?" I asked. She nodded. "I kinda want to be alone—to think about it," I said.

"Oh, sure, honey. That's understandable."

I wrote a note and set it on my bed. I wasn't going to eat my way through this one.

"I'm going for a drive," I said.

"Be careful, honey. Please," she sounded tired of saying that.

I grabbed two sleeping bags from the shed and put them in the car, then drove around the east side of the ranch and parked on the side of the road next to the creek bed, where I didn't think anyone ever drove. It was a long walk out to the barn from there, and I watched the cattle in the distance along the way. The barn's worn roof showed in the valley under the tree. *This time next week it won't be there*, I thought. I climbed the tree and saw Cody on the opposite side of the bluff, making his way across the plateau. The wind picked up in a gust and sent dust and gravel flying across the plain, bending down the dry, tall grass. Cody lifted his arms up to shield his face.

I didn't take my eyes off him. His lanky figure, his dark, greasy hair. As he got closer, he saw me and the half smile crossed his face. I climbed down, and dust pelted the back of my bare legs in the wind.

He walked straight toward me then stopped a foot away.

"What did you tell Sandy?" I asked.

He shrugged. "Nothing," he said. "What did you tell your parents?"

"I left a note. *Don't worry–I'm safe, but I'm not coming home until morning.*"

"You're brave," Cody laughed. Then his breath caught in his throat, and he gazed intently at the dirt for a moment. "Are you sure this is what you want to do? I mean–we don't have to *do* anything. We can just–or whatever you want," he changed his gaze to study the clouds. "I just mean–being gone all night long and everything–are you sure you want to do that?"

"I am absolutely sure," I said.

We sat by the tree and watched the sun set and ate the kind of chocolate donuts you get at the gas station for dinner. Then we washed it down with pop.

"Have you ever watched someone die?" I asked after the sun was all the way down.

"No," he said. "Was it scary?"

"No. I was scared at first, but then–it was peaceful."

"How do you feel now?"

"Sad. But–I feel bad, like I should just be sad–but I also feel alive."

Cody nodded. "After my uncle died—I was devastated. He was like my father. But I thought, I *have* to live—because he can't."

I got up, dusted my shorts off, and pulled Cody up by his hands. The wind had died down. I took his arms and wrapped them around my waist. I looked up at the tree, over at the barn, at the sky with the first stars appearing.

For the first time, I saw myself in focus.

I thought about Mr. Billy's poems. *I too am untranslatable.*

I laid my head on Cody's chest and listened to his heartbeat for a minute. It was beating sort of fast. We stood there together like that and watched the moon rise. It was waxing, on its way to becoming a harvest moon. The kind that looks like a big, orange earth rising up right next to us. The kind the farmers harvest the wheat by, and lovers warm themselves by, and dreamers write poems by. But that night it was still just a sliver.

"Let's go inside," I whispered.

We snuggled up on the sleeping bags and laid there for a while, letting the darkness close in around us, listening to the breeze blow through the slats and remembering when it was a tornado blowing through. We heard the chimes ringing every so often and some small critter scurrying around outside. Cody moved his hand that was around my lower back up to my front and very slowly started unbuttoning my shirt. I was wearing the same one I had on when we got caught in the twister.

"I don't want to end up like Missy or my mom," I whispered.

He stopped and pulled his hand away.

"That's why donuts and pop aren't the only things I got at the gas station," I added.

Cody's smile glowed in the dark barn.

"I got some too," he said. His hand went back to unbuttoning. Then he started kissing me in his soft, slow way that made me feel like pure love. I don't understand how Juan Pablo's priest could say he and Missy were pure sin if what they felt was the same as me at that moment.

Desire, I thought. *Desire is the path to God.* The desire to live in the everlasting love of His holiness. The desire to shake off the torments that bind us here on Earth. The desire to be one with God's love. Cody's body moved on top of mine. His neck tasted salty; his lips felt soft. His breath was like the beating wings of butterflies.

Was this the torment? Or was it the path to God?

Cody's hand moved down my chest and stomach and unbuttoned my shorts.

"Oh my God," I said.

"Are you cussing," he smiled, "or praying?"

"I don't know," I breathed.

He lifted up on his elbows, pushed my hair away from my face, and looked in my eyes for the longest time without speaking or moving.

"Stop thinking. Breathe," he said.

I did as he said and felt my chest push up against his.

"Now," he whispered, "do you want to do this?"

I closed my eyes and felt the length of his body stretching down along mine. I tried not to think, just to feel. When I opened my eyes, he was still looking at me, patient, calm. I felt heat rise up from the ground underneath me and spread through my body. I looked up through a hole in the roof and saw stars kissing stars.

"I've never been so sure about anything."

Then I stopped thinking. Wide strokes of understanding flooded through me. *The pieties of lovers' hands.*

I woke up to the sound of the meadowlarks singing. They were so loud. Cody was sleeping with his shirt balled up under his head as a pillow. Sunlight came through the east side of the barn, and somehow the light seemed changed. I waited until the sun hit Cody's face and woke him up.

He reached out and put his arms around my waist, pulling me toward him, kissing my back and shoulders.

"Can we stay here all day?" he asked.

"You can," I said. "I'm going to church."

17

THE FIGHT

Omnipresence. Dad's sermon was about omnipresence. God is everywhere all the time. He was trying to shame me, telling me God was watching Cody and me. Course He was. But it didn't make me feel ashamed.

The problem was Dad couldn't preach about God being everywhere all the time without also preaching that God's love was everywhere all the time too. He probably wished he was more of a fire-and-brimstone preacher that day, but he couldn't be, because that's not what he believed. He believed in God's omnipresent *love*. So, that's what he told us that morning. And for the first time, maybe for the first time ever, I really listened.

"*Praise God from Whom all blessings flow*," I sang with the congregation, "*Praise Him all creatures here below, Praise Him above ye Heavenly Host, Praise Father, Son, and Holy Ghost. Amen.*"

Music permeated my skin—and my blood and fibers and bones and cells and atoms—the music pulsed and vibrated me from the inside. I closed my eyes and let the familiar verse warm me. The collective breathing of the congregation. This is the comfort my parents chose to value above all else. I wondered in that moment if it was worth forsaking the rest of the world with its uncertainty and ugliness. And that act of wondering—just the question—set me apart from them.

I sat in the middle of the sanctuary surrounded by a shrinking congregation now that the weather wasn't quite so scorching. From my seat I could see the back of Mom's head up in the front row. I looked at her beautiful, soft hair. My hair. Her head remained bowed throughout most of the service, and I figured she was praying pretty hard—probably had been all night.

We stood up and sang the closing hymn. "You sure do have a pretty voice, Jesse," the lady next to me said as she picked up her purse. I didn't even know her name. "Glad to see you back." Mom shuffled out with the rest of the congregation and made small talk with the people who were leaving, then went downstairs to share the casseroles she had inevitably made the night before in an attempt to calm down and give her hands something to do.

Dad stood fixed at the pulpit, head bowed, with his hands gripping the sides of the podium until everyone but me had left the sanctuary.

I stayed in my seat.

He didn't say a thing. He didn't even look up.

I swallowed. "I'm sorry if I worried—"

"*We must not indulge in sexual immorality,*" he interrupted. He was reading from the Bible, his head still bowed down looking at it. "*If you think you are standing, watch out that you do not fall. No temptation has overtaken you that is not common to everyone.*" He lifted his eyes like it caused him a great deal of pain to look at me.

I didn't want to shrink away this time, but I could never find the words with him. So, I did what he always did. "Um," I cleared my throat, "*Hope does not put us to shame,*" I said, *"because God's love has been poured into our hearts through the Holy Spirit that has been given to us."*

"I'm not going to ask you where you were last night," he snapped. His knuckles turned white as he gripped the podium.

"Thank you," I said.

His face turned dark red, then purple, and I worried he had forgotten to breathe.

"Some things are just for me," I said.

"No." He hissed. "You live under *my* roof and you follow *my* rules." He released his grip on the podium and flipped through the Bible. "You are too young to have things just for you. You don't have secrets," he was still flipping pages, "you don't have hideouts. Freedom is *earned*, young lady."

My stomach churned, and I wanted to run away and not look back. Instead, I stood up.

"And from now on you don't have it until I say you have it," he went on.

I walked toward him. He was shaking. Shaking the way Sandy was when she had that gun pointed at Floyd.

"*Then the Lord answered Job out of the whirlwind,*" I said with weak breath, "*who is this that darkens counsel by words without knowledge?*" He looked injured, like I'd punched him. I found my breath, "*Have you comprehended the expanse of the Earth*?"

"How dare you use God's words against me!" he seethed.

"I'm not against you," I whispered.

"You will not drive anymore," he went on like I hadn't said a thing. "You will not go on *walks* without your mother or me. You will be home-schooled by your mother for the next year," he took a deep breath then, and leaned in close so I could hear his whisper, "and you will not so much as speak to, write to, or *think* about that boy—or any other boys like him."

"Like him? What's he like, Dad? Have you bothered to get to know him? Have you bothered to get to know me? *And God, who knows the human heart, has made no distinction between them and us."*

"You don't know what you're doing!" he pleaded, slamming the Bible closed. "Listen to me." He stepped down from the podium.

"I've been listening to you my whole life. Are you ever going to listen to me? I can't just stay here forever. I have movement in me."

"You have teenage infatuation in you and that is not something to make life choices with. Choices you will regret—"

"Like having me? That's what this is all about, right? You and Mom made a bad choice and it led to *me*—the biggest regret of your life. The thing that ruined it all."

He flinched. "You're a child, Jesse. You think you have it figured out—but you don't."

"I don't think I have anything figured out!" I cried. "But for the first time I want to—I'm trying. I'm trying to understand."

"But you don't listen! You don't listen for an instant!"

"God gave us these words so that we might comprehend the mystery of the *world,* Dad—not just comprehend *you.*"

"Can't you see you're slipping away, Jesse? You're slipping further and further from His love! I'm trying to protect you—I know how that feels."

"*His* love—or your love?" I asked. Dad was silent. "*Neither death, nor life, nor angels, nor rulers, nor things present, nor things to come, nor powers, nor height, nor depth, nor anything else in all creation, will be able to separate us from the love of God.* You taught me that, Dad. I listened."

My voice echoed against the sanctuary walls, and tears began to stream down my face.

"I've been trying my whole life to make you love me. To be a person you respect—to be who you think I should be," I said. "And I'm scared that you won't love me because of what I've done or how I think or what I feel. But I can't be your version of me anymore."

Dad blinked and pulled his head back. Then he whispered, "Jesse, there is nothing you could ever do, or think, or feel, that would make me stop loving you."

"You're against so many things, Dad," I whispered. "But what are you *for*?"

"Don't you know?" he asked. His lip shook and tears filled his eyes. "*You*, Jesse."

He took his handkerchief out, wiped his eyes and blew his nose.

"Your mother is so perfect, Jesse. Everyone loves her, and for some reason—I still don't know why—she chose me." He paused to place his handkerchief back in his pocket. "She was a dancer, when we were in high school. I saw her one afternoon practicing in the gym, and I lost my mind—that's why I know how you feel, Jesse." He turned his head and looked out the window. "I couldn't control my desires." He closed his eyes and shook his head. "When you were born, I looked at your feet and they were so small I thought you were missing a toe on each one. I ran to the doctor—I was worried that you only had eight toes. You were so helpless, Jesse, and I was so scared. I don't know why God ever trusted me to take care of you—I certainly don't deserve it—but I knew in that moment that your mom and I had to stop our sinful ways. For you. Don't you think I know I'm the good-for-nothing boy that ruined her life? I've been trying to make up for it for sixteen years." His face fell.

"You're still scared," I breathed, "aren't you?"

He furrowed his brow.

I took a deep breath. "*A thousand warbling echoes have started to life within me, never to die...Never again leave me to be the peaceful child I was before what there in the night, The unknown want...the destiny of me.*" I took a step toward Dad and squared my shoulders. “I don’t want to be to blame for your choices. And I don’t want you to be to blame for mine. I don’t want to feel guilty for ruining your life and your plans. I was a baby, and I don’t want to have come from sin—I want to come from love.”

18

SPINDRIFT LOVE

Dad preaches a lot about redemption. It's not like he goes around talking about it when we're eating dinner or playing cards or anything. People think because he's a minister he's always holy, even when he's mowing the lawn. But up there in front of the congregation he talks about redemption all the time. And forgiveness. But, like Cody said, I never learned it until I felt it.

Mom was at the stovetop, making fudge, when I walked in the door.

"What's the occasion?" I asked.

"Oh, fudge just makes you feel good inside," she answered.

"You know, you can't solve everything with food," I said.

She looked at me with a face that said, *of course you can,* but under her breath she muttered, "I know."

"You want me to bring this sun tea in?" I asked.

"*Do* you want me. No, honey, it needs more time. More time." She returned her focus to the pot in front of her.

"Do you know what happens to sugar when you heat it? The molecules break down into something simpler, then they form again into a completely different molecule. It loses part of the very thing that made it sugar, but then turns into something new. Still sweet. But different." Mom pushed a wooden spoon around the pot, scraping the melting fudge off the sides.

"Wanna taste?" she held out the spoon to me. I took it and licked the chocolate off the same way I had since I could hold a spoon.

"We know something you don't know, Dad and me." Mom took a spatula out of the drawer beside me. "Because we know what it feels like to love you, to be changed by that love." She began pouring the hot fudge from the pot into a glass casserole dish. "We're faking it a little, you know. Going about our day as if our hearts aren't breaking every moment. Pretending to be overwhelmed by work or chores when we're really overwhelmed by our own fragility. By the fact that our every breath depends on your well-being. That our hearts no longer exist inside our bodies–they are walking around, playing on the swings, going to school, running across the prairie." She placed the dish in the refrigerator and turned to me.

"Sacrifice is such a negative word for young people. But you'll never truly love without it. Or know what you're capable of. I'd do anything to learn what you have taught me: unconditional love." Mom took the spoon, now licked clean, out of my hand and set it in the pot, then left both of them to soak in the sink.

She walked to the front porch and lifted the sun tea off the stoop, holding it up in the afternoon light to check if it was done. I followed her and sat down on the swing. A long train was making its way, real slow, across the yard, creaking and moaning over the tracks.

"Will you braid my hair?" I asked.

"You don't really have much left to braid," she said, setting the tea back down. "I have a better idea." She went inside and put a record on. "Serenade," Schubert. Then she came out and took me by the hand. "Come on," she said, "I'm going to teach you how to dance."

She placed my left hand on her shoulder and took my right one in her hand. She started counting. "One two three. One two three."

Her right hand gently pushed my left hip to the right, her left hand pulled my arm in the same direction. Then she switched and moved me to the left.

"One two three, one two three," she lifted up slightly on the one and dipped down on the three.

I tried to follow her, I tried to count, but I was too shocked by what was happening. She attempted to spin us around then burst out laughing when I tripped over my own feet. She broke loose of me then, let me stand there, speechless, while she swayed across the front porch, spinning and rising, falling and reaching with the music. A look of complete contentment swept across her face. Her arms reached out above and around her like barn swallows climbing and diving for evening bugs. Her legs looked so strong, carrying her across the dusty, wooden planks, transforming our porch into a ballroom. Her body moved with a confidence that didn't care how pretty it looked, or how well it cooked, or what people it was bound to.

She wasn't following steps anymore. She was dancing a form that came from inside her. Her face became red and sweat wet her hair at the temples. When the song ended she looked at me with pure joy.

"Mom..." Tears streamed down my face.

She breathed for a few moments, then sat down on the swing and patted it for me to sit next to her.

"Do you forgive Dad for stopping you from dancing all this time?" I asked.

"Forgiveness is a path, not a destination. I came home one night—after you left, and he was standing at the sink doing the dishes. I stood back and watched him before he knew I was there. Watched the muscles in his forearm, scrubbing the pans. Watched his dry elbows as he rolled his sleeves up. Watched him gulp down his glass of tea—not wanting to waste any—before cleaning the glass out. He's a good man, your dad. And he didn't even bat an eye when it came to forgiving me."

I pushed the swing back gently. "Hey, look," I said, pulling a cicada shell from the side of the house. "I just had a thought—I'll be seventeen my next birthday. The seventeen-year cicadas were born when I was in your belly. They've been waiting my whole life to fly away."

"Let's go check on the fudge," she said.

Dad came home and we ate fudge for dinner because it was "good for the soul." We held hands around the table while Dad prayed. I closed my eyes and listened—to the slight uncertainty in his voice, to the fragility of his words. I cleared my throat.

"I applied to some colleges," I said casually, "while I was at Sandy's."

Dad looked up but didn't speak.

"And a few of them have invited me to come audition."

"Audition? I don't understand," Mom said.

"I applied to music programs. To study music. I wrote an essay about my ear and the twister and—I can go audition. For a scholarship."

"Audition how?" Dad asked.

"Singing," I said. "I might be able to get a scholarship by singing."

Mom and Dad stared at me. Then they looked at each other.

"I have to leave tomorrow if I'm going to make it back in time for school to start."

"Where?" Dad asked it slowly, like if he drew it out long enough the answer wouldn't come.

"By the ocean."

"There is *no* way you are driving *all* the way—"

"Have you lost your *mind*? Absolutely not—"

Mom and Dad talked over each other. I stood up, and they went silent.

"I'm going," I said.

Dad almost laughed. "Jesse, how are you going to do that? There's no way the Brown Bomber could make it to California."

"Cody fixed it up. He says it'll make it."

"What are you talking about?" Mom looked genuinely scared.

"I used the money from my internship to buy parts and stuff and Cody fixed it for me. It'll get me there and back."

"Even if that's true," Dad hesitated, "what if something goes wrong? Do you know how to change a flat tire, or—"

"I sure do, Dad. And change the oil and even the brake pads." I smiled at the surprised looks on their faces and added quietly, "You don't have to be scared of this. I can do it."

They stared in silence for a few moments. I reached down to take another bite of fudge.

"No," Dad said finally. "You can't drive across the country by yourself, Jesse. You just can't."

"I know I can," I said. "But—" I held up my hand to stop them from talking so I could finish, "but if Mom wants to come along, that would be okay too."

They looked at each other.

"I thought you'd be happy," I said. "If I just close my eyes and sing like I'm in church, I could go to a real college."

"No, honey," Mom said, taking a deep breath. "Don't sing like you're in church. Sing like you're in the barn."

Cody was waiting for me where the road dead-ends up on the plateau. His Chevelle was ready to go, had been for a while, and now he was too.

"How am I going to figure things out without you to talk to?" I asked, my head against his shoulder, breathing in his scent as long as I could, trying to commit it to memory.

"There's no such thing as having things figured out," he smiled.

"The barn goes down tomorrow," I said, and flashes of our night there flew across my eyes. The inside of my body surged so strongly it surprised me.

"Are you gonna watch?" Cody asked. "Do you want me to stay and go with you?"

"No, I want to remember it intact." His half smile crept across my face, then his.

"I have a present for you," he said. He reached into the trunk and pulled out a wooden box.

The moment I saw it I knew what it was: slats from the barn. I held it in my hands and leaned down to smell it.

"I made it from pieces that were blown off in the tornado," he said.

"It's the most perfect present in the world," I said. "Thank you."

"Open it."

I lifted the lid and found compartments with lids and boxes within boxes, all made from barn wood. And tucked away in secret drawers were pieces of me: Prairie grass braids; nails from the wind chimes; sweet, dry hay; cotton from the cottonwoods; Mr. Billy's book; pebbles from the creek; a dried sunflower; and a lock of Cody's hair, tied up with prairie grass. I picked it up and breathed it in.

We stood there, looking out over the prairie where the twister chased us toward each other. Cody grabbed both my hands and pulled them up close to his chest.

"Thanks for saving my life," I said.

He looked down at the scar on his arm. "Hey, no problem,"

he shrugged.

"I don't just mean that," I said, running my hand along the scar.

"Tell me what you think after you see it," he said.

"See what?"

"The ocean."

He leaned his head down and pressed his forehead and nose against mine and took a long breath.

"*Bind us in time, O Seasons clear*," he recited, "*and awe*."

Then he melted away from me.

It rained.

Soft, sweet rain that the entire county had been praying for in one form or another all summer long. It felt like tears falling over me, mixing with mine. It felt like a million tiny feathers trailing down my arms and back, coolness after being pulled out of the fire, a bandage around my wounds. It felt like the second coming.

I walked home through it, carrying my box. I took my time and let it soak me through and through. The earth soaked it up too. It fell so softly that the cracked and broken dirt had time to take it in, to carry it down to the deep places where the roots were starving.

It was the best thing I've ever smelled. The sweet grass, the earth so rough and seasoned.

And it sounded like a whisper bouncing off the door of the prairie. I listened as hard as I could, hoping to hear the wisdom of it. But the sound was so beautiful I couldn't get past my joy at hearing it to listen to what was said underneath.

I walked in rhythm with the music of the rain, marking time with my shoulders. I thought about my shoulders smiling, other parts of my body hearing, questioning, sighing.

I reached the edge of the ridge, where I could look out and see the top of my cottonwood. The sky to the west took on a pale blue color. The rain continued to fall as part of the sky cleared, revealing pink clouds. I took out Mr. Billy's book and read it out loud to the setting sun. I didn't think he would mind if it got wet.

"O Minstrel galleons of Carib fire, bequeath us to no earthly shore—"

The lower the sun dropped, the redder and oranger the light became. The pale blue streaked with giant, blood-red shafts of light. Orange and pink and yellow crept up slowly behind it and reflected in the misty rain.

"Until is answered in the vortex of our grave, the seal's wide, spindrift gaze toward paradise."

I closed the book, and right at that moment the monarchs rose up out of the milkweeds. The granddaughters and grandsons of the monarchs I'd seen three months ago. They were feeding on the same milkweeds their grandparents had fed on, this time making their way back down to Mexico for the winter. They fluttered in front of the burning sky and spread out over the prairie grass. They quickened again inside me.

I had it then. My own spindrift gaze. I've never loosened my grip on it.

Some think love is a feeling that settles in to live inside of us—or floats in one day and then floats out again, just as easily.

But I know it's a force.

Stronger than a twister. Shifting mountains. Carving canyons.

Lifting up the sea.

ACKNOWLEDGEMENTS

Thank you to my gravity, my Martijn. Thank you to my unwaveringly supportive (and patient) family, near and far. Thank you, Chazz Glaze, for saving this manuscript, and my artist's soul, from the fire. Thank you to the brilliant and merciful José Moreira. Thank you to the creative and compassionate Eric Moore. Thank you, Jasper and Whitman, for being exactly who you are. Thank you to Trista Edwards and everyone at Atmosphere Press. And thank you, Professor Marty Bickman, for assigning to me, the nine-month word.

ABOUT ATMOSPHERE PRESS

ABOUT THE AUTHOR

photo by @vernajordan

Jocelyn lives in Colorado where she sleeps under a couple cats; plays the singing saw with her band, 2 Star Hotel; explores the world with her drummer; and loves, above all, reading with her two children every night.

CPSIA information can be obtained
at www.ICGtesting.com
Printed in the USA
BVHW090128130722
641608BV00004B/23